On a Whim

On a Whim

A Thurston Hotel Novel:
Book 3

Win Day

ON A WHIM

ISBN 978-0-9952082-1-6

Copyright © 2016 by Win Day
Published by Creative Implementations
106 Garrison Square SW
Calgary, Alberta T2T 6B2
Canada

Also available in electronic edition
ISBN 978-0-9952082-0-9

NOTE TO READERS

The Thurston Hotel Novels were the brainchild of our project mom, Brenda Sinclair, who also wrote the opening and closing books of the collection. When she initially invited all of us to hop on board her Thurston Hotel idea train, none of us could have foreseen either the amount of work involved or the amount of fun we would have. And it has been so much fun!

The Thurston Hotel is located on Main Street in our fictional mountain resort town of Harmony, nestled in the foothills of the Canadian Rockies. While working with our plotlines and coordinating our characters and settings with the other authors' stories, everyone started to believe the town of Harmony, Alberta was actually on the map. (Sorry, readers, it's not.)

I hope you enjoy reading this book as much as I enjoyed writing it.

Be sure to check out the rest of the collection!

And happy reading!

DEDICATION

To my fellow Thurston Hotel authors,
who have worked so tirelessly to create this collection:
Thank you. I have learned from all of you.

To Paula Chaffee Scardamalia,
first my book coach, now my critique partner,
always my friend:
Your help and inspiration make me a better writer.
Thank you. This is the first book of many.

To my husband, Tom Day:
You are my hero, every day. I couldn't do this without you.
Thanks for everything.

Chapter One

The last thing Mandy Brighton needed at seven o'clock on a cold March morning was to get trapped in the alley between her business and the building next door by a herd of elk.

Closing her eyes, she thunked her head against the headrest, once, twice, and then again for good measure. She straightened up and whimpered when she looked out the windshield. Yes, they were still there. And now she was going to be late.

"I love this place, really I do," she muttered under her breath as she fumbled for the cell phone in her purse on the passenger seat. She truly did, most days. The cute little tourist town snuggled into the foothills of the Rockies boasted gorgeous mountain scenery, a busy Main Street with rows of vintage buildings housing quirky local shops like hers, and a stately historic hotel down the block.

It also boasted wildlife that occasionally wandered through the town center and brought traffic to a halt.

She dialed the shop's number and waited impatiently until her assistant picked up. "Kelsey? Hey, can you—"

"Where are you? Did you forget something?"

"No, listen. I need you to grab a big metal bowl and a wooden spoon or something, and go out the front door and bang loudly as you come toward the alley."

The silence from her assistant was deafening.

"Please tell me we don't have a bear trying to get into the garbage bins again," the other woman said warily.

"Not a bear. Elk."

Mandy heard the clatter as Kelsey grabbed a bowl from the ever-present stack in the kitchen, then the jingle of the sleigh bells hanging inside the front door as her friend stepped outside.

The herd surrounding her minivan noticed the banging as soon as she did. Their heads snapped to attention, and as one they spun and trotted away from the street and into the parking lot behind the building. The last of them rounded the corner as Kelsey peered cautiously into the alleyway that ran between Whimsy, Mandy's cupcake bakery, and the next row of storefronts.

Mandy threw her van in gear and crunched over last night's fresh snow, before coming to a stop and rolling down her window. "Thanks, Kels. I didn't want to honk the horn and scare them. Remember what they did to that tourist last month?"

"Oh, yeah, I think the rental car company wrote off his car." Kelsey shivered in the frosty morning. Until the sun rose higher, the alley would be in deep shadow. March had come in like a lion this year, as the late February blizzards extended into steady snowfalls and unseasonable cold.

"Go, go! I've got to get to the Chamber of Commerce breakfast. See you later!"

Snow-covered sidewalks ran along the two blocks of freshly plowed streets between her parking lot and the

Thurston Hotel. Mandy tapped her horn and waved at Gill, the bellhop, as she drove past the front door and around the side of the hotel to the service entrance. Gill met her vehicle as she pulled up, and helped her unload onto her trolley. Today's deliveries included the regular assortment of cookies and cupcakes and specialty desserts for the hotel coffee shop and restaurant, as well as cupcakes for the Chamber meeting. The two of them made short work of stacking the shiny white pastry boxes. Mandy smiled to see the fastidious Gill carefully line them all up to show her shop's logo, which had swirly green lettering that said "Whimsy: Cupcakes, Celebration Cakes, and Specialty Desserts" and her address and phone number next to a drawing of a yellow cupcake with pink frosting.

"Big delivery today," Gill commented as she slid home the van door. "I'll park your van if you save me a cupcake!"

"I've got one right here with your name on it," she promised, pointing to the smallest box on the top of the stack. "I'll leave it behind the valet station for you. And thanks!"

Most of her haul went to Guy LaFontaine, the very French head chef already at work in the basement kitchen.

"Full crowd in the Ptarmigan Room already for the Chamber meeting," he told her as he signed for the delivery. "Want to leave your trolley down here and pick it up after, *chérie*?"

"Thanks, Chef—see you later!"

3

Mandy dropped off her boxes of cupcakes at the breakfast buffet spread out at one end of the meeting room, then filled her plate before wandering to a chair. She greeted half a dozen friends before taking a seat next to Wendy Thurston, the hotel's events manager and Chamber secretary.

"Wow, the place is packed this morning," Mandy observed as she poured herself a cup of coffee. "Even Mayor Hamilton is here. What's up?"

"We're announcing a silent auction as part of the campaign to raise funds for the community playground," Wendy replied. "Katherine Keeler of Sleek Chic is heading it up. I hope you'll contribute."

"Sure. I can donate... How about a fancy dinner for two, catered at the winner's home: four, maybe five courses, including a selection of desserts?"

"Sounds terrific! I didn't know Whimsy did catering. Don't you only make cakes and cupcakes and desserts?"

Mandy quickly swallowed her mouthful of scrambled eggs. "I don't do a lot yet. Don't have room. But the yarn shop next to Whimsy might fold into the quilt shop next to them, which means that middle bay will be up for grabs. I want to take it over and put a little café in the front, maybe a dozen, fifteen tables, and expand up into the apartments above the two shops to add a commercial kitchen that can also do some catering. Box lunches for skiers and hikers, romantic dinners for the culinarily challenged, that sort of thing."

"Big plans! Anyone else know about this?" Wendy asked.

"My lawyer and my accountant. And my great-aunt, of course. I'm waiting to see if the space opens up. I can move pretty quick if it does. Don't say anything, okay?"

"Before you make any decisions, make sure you listen to the other part of today's presentation. You know the architect hired for the town hall renovations and the new community center?" Wendy pointed discreetly to a man sitting with the mayor, near the podium at the front. "According to the mayor, he's got some sort of plan to 'revitalize Main Street', I think they called it. He presented it to the town council on Friday."

"I didn't know we needed to revitalize Main Street," Mandy said.

"Me neither. But I heard it's a pretty impressive plan."

"We had to scramble to get the infrastructure funds for the town hall and community center. And we're fundraising for the playground. Even if it is a good plan, where would the money come from?"

"No idea." Wendy looked up as Dory Berholtz, the current president of the Chamber and the owner of Dory's Clip and Curl, called the meeting to order. "Anyway, I'll catch you later. I have to take attendance and the minutes." As she stood and gathered up her notes, she said, "Be sure to enter your dinner into the silent auction when the form comes around!"

The meeting started as usual for their small town's Chamber of Commerce: round-robin introductions, a new face or two, and then Katherine's presentation on the fundraiser to collect thirty thousand dollars for the new playground. During the break, Mandy chatted with the other members at her table, passed business cards to a new guy from one of the car dealers in town, then refilled her coffee before settling in to listen to the featured presentation.

Dory rose from her chair and gazed around the room. "Could we resume our meeting now, please? It's our pleasure to have Mayor Hamilton here this morning. And he comes with a special duty. Mr. Hamilton, please introduce our guest speaker." She settled back into her seat at the end of the table.

Ed Hamilton approached the podium and adjusted the microphone for his taller stance. "Good morning, ladies and gentlemen. It's great to see such an enthusiastic turnout from our local businesses at such an early hour. As many of you already know, this is Kevin MacNeal, the architect who designed the town hall renovations and the beautiful new community center. Our successful application for grant funding has enabled us to think a little bigger. And Kevin is just the man for the job..."

Mandy tuned out a little when the silent auction sign-up sheet arrived in front of her. Ed could be a little long-winded, she knew. She filled out her entry for an "elegant gourmet dinner for two" and passed the form on to the next person, then turned back toward the podium as Kevin, or

Kenneth or whatever his name was, showed a slide of an artist's rendering of a slick, modern streetscape up on the screen: his concept for Main Street.

Mandy almost choked. *Main Street? That's not my Main Street.* It didn't look like any street in Harmony. It didn't look like any street in any small town, in her opinion.

Kevin MacNeal delivered his practiced spiel about "modernizing Main Street" and "bringing Harmony into the twenty-first century" and "opening opportunities for new franchises, new money" that would "make Harmony a real destination" in the foothills of the Rockies.

Mandy divided her attention between him and the crowd. Some of the audience, most notably the big car dealers, a couple of the accountants and investment councilors, and a guy from the bank branch around the corner from Whimsy, looked suitably impressed.

But the faces of many of the others—the owners of the ski hill and the golf course, the rep from the Wobbly Dog, a local pub, even Katherine and Dory—showed expressions ranging from mild distaste to outright horror. Wendy looked appalled.

The presentation ended to scattered applause. When the speaker opened the floor for questions, Mandy's hand shot up first.

He ignored her, responding to the men sitting closest to the podium: the ones who had evidently appeared to support the planned development. Most of the questions focused on what franchises might become available, what big chain stores and eateries Harmony might be able to attract. How much money it might mean to them in the long run.

No one asked the questions she wanted to hear. And she grew tired of being overlooked.

Mandy stood. At the next lull, she asked loudly, "Where exactly is this development site planned for? Because if I recall correctly, there aren't any empty building lots along Main Street."

"And you are?" the architect asked, his eyes tracking first to her face, then down to the nametag pinned prominently to her blazer, then back to her face. If he didn't already know who she was, her nametag—a yellow cupcake with pink frosting and her name emblazoned on it in swirly pink letters—made it clear what kind of shop she represented.

"Mandy Brighton. I own Whimsy, the cupcake shop on Main."

"Ah. Yes, of course. As you can see," he replied, turning back to his laptop and bringing back one of the earlier slides, "we're looking at redeveloping the lot across the street and a block to the east of the hotel. It's—"

"Why?"

"I'm sorry, what?"

"*Why* do you want to redevelop that block? And you're not proposing to renovate the existing buildings, you're talking about knocking them down and building *that*." She pointed at the screen, once again showing the artist's rendition of a large new mixed-use retail-commercial-residential building. "Why?"

"Well, because, because…"

She almost felt sorry for him. He looked confused as to why anyone could possibly object to his plans. But sympathy only went so far: that was *her* building he wanted to rip down!

"Because Harmony could attract new investment, new businesses! It would mean getting some big-city advantages in your small town."

"But you're not talking about bringing in new businesses and putting them into a spot where we might need new businesses. You're talking about destroying existing businesses, successful ones, to make room for others. Businesses that might not succeed here."

"Yes, but they'd be new! In a new building! Think how attractive that would be."

"Attractive to who? My customers are a mix of locals and tourists. The tourists come here to get away from the big city. The locals stay here because it's not the big city. So who would these new businesses be attractive to?"

"Well, to other businesses, of course. And to the tourists who pass through on their way into the Rockies. They're used to the familiar. They—"

"They like the small-town atmosphere, at least for a visit. Plus, I'm pretty sure we have development restrictions in place to prevent those big chains from opening in town. So unless the Planning and Development board has changed the rules without telling anyone? Yes? No?" Mandy looked around the room, trying to make eye contact with some of those board members. A couple of them frowned and shook their heads at her, which she interpreted as no support for this crazy plan. But a few, a significant few, wouldn't meet her gaze.

"And I'm sorry, but that's all the time we have today," interrupted Ed Hamilton. "Kevin, thank you for presenting your plan for the revitalization of our Main Street. I see we have some community outreach to do before we formally bring it before Planning and Development." He nodded in Mandy's direction, then deftly steered the architect away from the podium, saying, "Thank you, Chamber, for inviting us today. You know my office is open at any time, should anyone want more information or to continue this discussion."

The chair adjourned the meeting, and Mandy lost Kevin and the mayor in the crowd as the attendees dispersed. She was too short to see over heads, and too polite to elbow her way through. And half the crowd wanted to talk to her about this new development.

Opinion was split. The owner of the big Ford dealership on the edge of town was decidedly in favor, as were the gas station and convenience store folks. The small, family-owned businesses, whether located on her stretch of Main Street or elsewhere, not so much.

She finally found Ed Hamilton and his architect as they were leaving. "Ed! Could I have a word?"

"Mandy! Good to see you. I understand Riley and Brock have an appointment later this week to talk wedding cakes. Kevin," he said, turning to the younger man, "this is Mandy Brighton. She owns—"

"Whimsy, the cupcake place. So I heard. Ms. Brighton, if you're interested in an explanation of the financial projections for the project, I can—"

"No, thanks anyway. I'm sure you've run your numbers. But you haven't seen mine. I own a successful business, Mr. MacNeal, and one I intend to keep operating in its present location. There's been a family-owned bakery in that spot since the Schmidt building opened in 1914."

"But don't you see? That's the thing. The building is quite old. If it's anything like a lot of older buildings in small towns like this, it's due for major renovations. I'm sure the owners would be open to a purchase offer, a generous purchase offer. After all, it's just real estate to them. If they wanted to get in as investors in the new development, I'm sure there will be opportunities."

Oh, so now her building needed major renovations? "Mr. MacNeal, have you been in any of the stores in that strip? Or in the buildings that face the other streets and share our parking lot?"

"I don't need to. I've done enough of these projects to know old buildings outlive their usefulness. Better materials of construction, updated building codes, new safety regulations: there are a lot of reasons to tear down and rebuild. The owners—"

"And have you spoken to them? Do you even know who owns the building?"

"I understand it's the Schmidt Family Corporation. I have to find out from their lawyer who the corporate contact person is, and then we'll sit down and discuss the sale."

"Good luck with that," Mandy said. "Pretty sure you'll have to go through the Anderson & Anderson Law Firm. I doubt the owners will be interested in talking to you about selling."

"And you know this because…?"

"It's a small town, Mr. MacNeal. Everyone knows everyone here. Anderson & Anderson handles the rent checks for our building, but the tenants all know who actually owns it. And seriously, don't get your hopes up about a possible sale. Or about getting development permits for big chains."

She flashed him her fiercest smile as she spun on her heel and headed for the door. So Mr. Big-City Architect thought he'd be able to convince the local commercial real estate owners to sell out? Or convince enough members of the Planning and Development board, or the town council, to let in the big chains they've been fighting off for years? "Don't be so sure," she muttered as she took the stairs down to the lobby.

Chapter Two

Mandy closed the door to her walk-in fridge with more force than necessary. A good night's sleep hadn't been enough to calm her down.

Her assistant glanced up from where she was piping green peppermint frosting onto vanilla butter cupcakes. "Hey, be careful. We want these beautiful, right? Don't make me miss and make a mess!"

"Sorry, Kels. I was thinking…"

"I know. About those plans to tear down your building," Kelsey replied, her attention once more on the careful swirls of colored frosting over pale cake. She finished the one she held and reached up and rubbed her chin with the back of her hand. "Or are you thinking about the architect?"

"What? No! Not the way you mean, anyway. I wonder why we've never seen him in here, that's all. He's been in town now for what, two months? And he's staying at the Thurston Hotel, working at the town hall site down the block, and he doesn't pop in for coffee and a cupcake? We see most of the site-prep crew every day. Sometimes twice a day!" Mandy groused as she set the butter and eggs on the worktable in the middle of the kitchen and went to collect the rest of the ingredients.

That worktable was the heart of the kitchen, and came from the original bakery fixtures: a holdover from generations past. As she walked by on her way to the storage cupboards, she ran her hand lovingly over the stainless steel, admiring the overhead light reflected in its shiny surface, only slightly marred by nicks and dimples left by years of use.

"I'd say it meant he isn't a coffee drinker, except I know from the guys he is. They say he was so annoyed there's no Starbucks in downtown Harmony, he went back to Calgary to get his own fancy schmancy espresso machine. He runs back to his hotel suite two, three times a day to make his own coffee." Kelsey frowned in concentration as she gave the piping bag her signature little flip and twist, putting a decorative peak on the top of the last cupcake in front of her. "Grab me the shamrocks, would you?"

"Sure." Mandy grabbed one of their rolling racks and made the rounds of the kitchen, gathering all her ingredients and adding a tray of Kelsey's gumdrop shamrocks. "These are cute. I'm glad you like making candy. These look so much better than the ones you can buy," she commented as she placed the tray within Kelsey's reach.

"I'm surprised you don't like to make candy, because you love the fancy cake decorating. But I'm glad you don't because I do!" replied her friend. "Tell me what you've got going there. I didn't think we had any specialty cakes scheduled this week."

"No orders on the board, but I've got the Hamilton-Anderson tasting tomorrow, and I want to give Riley and Brock a bunch of samples to choose from. Going to make four small cakes, half a dozen fillings, and three or four frostings to show different flavors and decorating techniques." Mandy pulled over a bowl and started separating eggs.

"Oh, and you don't think Lilith Hamilton is going to drive that bus? She'll want either a white cake with white fondant or a traditional fruitcake with marzipan."

"Nope, not fruitcake. No nuts, including almonds. Which leaves out that really great walnut cake too. But you're right about the white frosting, white cake for Lilith. I'm hoping I can talk Riley into something a little more adventurous."

Kelsey snorted as she placed the finished cupcakes onto the serving tray sized to fit in the glass display cases out front. "Good luck with that. And getting back to our original topic of discussion for this afternoon, what do you think about our hottie architect?"

"Other than he's a brand snob who will never know the delights of the best cupcakes and pastries in town, since he never comes in here? I don't think anything about him at all."

"Liar." Kelsey snatched the rolling rack from next to Mandy and loaded up her trays of cupcakes. "I can find out more for you if you want, you know."

"Oh, yeah? How?"

"She'll ask her adoring public," came a young voice from the swinging double doors leading into the front of the shop. Mandy's newest part-time employee, Suzette Sheridan, held the doors while Kelsey pushed the rack into the front, then came in and plopped onto the stool next to Mandy.

"Her adoring public?"

"You know, all the construction guys. They ask for her every afternoon when they come in around now. Can I help?" she asked, indicating the piles of ingredients.

"Sure, you can get the butter softening. I've marked which recipes I'm making. I'll do a small round layer of each, enough for a tasting," Mandy instructed, sliding over her binder of recipes. She frowned at the door swinging shut behind Kelsey's exit with her trays of cupcakes. "They do know she's married, right?"

"Oh, sure, married with kids. They ask to see baby pictures. I think that's why they like to flirt with her. It's safe."

"Huh. Who knew?" Mandy shook her head as she started to measure out the dry ingredients for the first cake.

"Wise beyond her years, that's our Suzette." Kelsey breezed back into the kitchen, her rolling rack now full of empty trays. "Listen, Mandy, the guys have about the same opinion of Mr. Hottie Architect as you do: he's a stuck-up city snob who doesn't think much of small towns or the people who live here."

"I bet they don't call him Mr. Hottie, though!" Suzette laughed as she finished measuring all the butter into the various mixing bowls and moved on to the other wet ingredients.

Mandy pulled on the spring-loaded shelf under the worktable, something she added during her renovations, to raise one of her stand mixers up to the counter level. After locking the shelf in place, she reached for a bowl containing some butter. "This one for the eggnog cake?"

"Umm, yes. That's the right one. I don't think I've had that one, have I?"

"Probably not," Mandy said. She had to raise her voice over the noise of the mixer. "I haven't used it for cupcakes in a while. It's a good cake recipe, though."

"And we all know you make the best cakes—which our not-so-friendly architect will never realize because he refuses to come by and taste one," said Kelsey. Her eyes lit up. "I know!"

"Know what?"

"You should send him cupcakes anyway. Send them with the guys; they'll deliver for you. Bribe him with treats till he comes to see you in person. Then you should seduce him!"

"Seduce him? Are you nuts? I don't even like him! And you shouldn't say stuff like that in front of Suzette."

"She's a big girl, she's heard worse. And why do you have to like him? You just have to sleep with him." Kelsey sounded more enthusiastic the more she spoke. "No, really! Seducing him is a great idea. You haven't had a date in ages, and maybe he'd fall for you and then he won't want to tear down your building!"

"You *are* nuts." Mandy added the sugar to the creamed butter and kept mixing. "Seriously. I don't know where you get these ideas. Don't listen to her," she advised the rapt Suzette. "And don't ever go to her for dating advice either."

"Oh, I don't know." The younger girl giggled. "It sounds like a good plan to me!"

"See? She agrees with me! I bet Zak would agree with me too. Want me to ask him?"

"No! This crazy idea never leaves this kitchen, okay? Sheesh." She reached for the rest of the dry ingredients and slowly began to add them to the mixture in her bowl.

"You know, I bet your Auntie Anna would agree you should go for it. If she was forty years younger, she'd chase after him herself!"

"Don't be ridiculous. Forty years ago Auntie Anna was happily married." Mandy poured the cake batter into the prepared pan and bounced it a few times to remove any air bubbles. She carried it over to the bank of wall ovens, then slid the pan in the top one and set the timer. "I can't believe you're still going on about this."

"Does she know he wants to tear the building down?"

"If she does, she didn't hear it from me. These days she doesn't get involved in any of the corporate management stuff unless I ask for her opinion or advice about something. And I'm more likely to ask about recipes than real estate!"

"I still think we should ask Zak," Kelsey grumbled. She squirted the last of the icing from the piping bag onto a tasting spoon and ate it before gathering her decorating equipment to wash it in the big sink.

"Ask me what?" Zak poked his head around the doorframe. "Mandy, phone up front."

"Inquiring minds want to know if you think Mandy should go after this Kevin MacNeal guy and seduce him so he stops chasing after her building and starts chasing after her!" Kelsey spoke loudly to be heard over the running water.

Mandy glared at her assistant as she hopped off her stool and exited the kitchen. "Give it a rest, Kels."

She slid behind the long counter in the front of her bakery, smiling and nodding at the Harmony Construction guys milling around in her little seating area, bumping into each other. *I really need the extra space; hope the bay next door empties out soon.* She picked up the phone. "Hello, this is Mandy Brighton of Whimsy, how can I help you?"

CLICK. The sound of the disconnect reverberated from the phone

"Well, that was rude." She pulled the receiver away from her ear, pressed "Off," and returned it to the charging stand.

"Another hang-up?" Zak stood behind the counter, packing up a box of six for one of the carpenters.

Mandy chuckled. She never tired of seeing these big, burly guys delicately peel the white paper stamped with her swirly green logo from a cupcake before downing it in a bite or two.

"What do you mean, another hang-up? Are we getting a lot?" She moved beside him to take orders and run the register, freeing him to pack faster.

"I don't know if it's a lot, but we got one or two every day this week. There you go, Ron, enjoy! Hey, Ron, how come that new guy, the architect, never comes in here?"

"Dunno. We figure he's too stuck up to come here even though you have great coffee and amazing desserts. Almost as good as the scenery!" The older man grinned and winked at Mandy. They all laughed when she blushed.

"No, seriously, guys, how can we get him in here to try us out? You know he wants to tear down the building, right?" Mandy glanced around the crowd.

"He can't do that! Can he do that?"

"What will you do if you have to move out? Is there someplace else in town you can go?"

"Could you lease a spot in the new building?"

The questions came fast and furious from the crowd.

"Hold on, hold on! I'm not going anywhere. Whimsy isn't going anywhere! You'll always be able to get your cupcake fix. Besides," she informed them, "he can't boot me out. He doesn't know it yet, but I own the building."

Chapter Three

"Here's the luggage cart. Do you need help getting all this inside?"

"No, that's OK, Gill, I can manage from here. I appreciate the cart, though," Mandy said to the helpful bellhop. "Somehow it didn't seem like this much when I packed up at the shop, or I would have brought my own trolley. I'll bring the cart back after the tasting, I promise." She waved as they parted company just inside the service entrance.

Loaded up as it was with her sample cakes, containers of fillings and frostings, binders of specialty cake styles, boxes of decorations, and laptop, the cart bumped heavily as she wheeled it out of the service elevator. The front wheel caught as she moved from the marble-floored hallway over the edge of the carpet in the lobby. Mandy swore under her breath and lunged to steady the stack when it threatened to topple over.

A pair of hands grabbed the front of the cart and helped her guide it over the bump. "Here, let me help you."

Together they eased the cart onto the rug. "Thanks," she said, peeking around the cart to face her rescuer, Kevin MacNeal. "I— Oh, I didn't expect you." The little buzz of nerves running up her arms and shoulders caught her by surprise. *And what's that all about?* She glanced at the old grandfather clock chiming for four o'clock "Ended a little early today?"

"Now, Mandy, I know you were raised better than that," chided a lovely old woman as she came out of the gift shop. "What would your great-aunt say about those manners?" Mrs. Arbuckle, the elderly resident of one of the sixth-floor suites, shook her head with a smile.

"Sorry, Mrs. A. And I apologize to you too," she said to Kevin. "That was uncalled for."

"No worries. We did finish early today. Where are you taking all this?"

"Across the lobby and into the Margaret Library. I've got it now, thanks," Mandy said, trying to pull the cart away from him. The closer she stood to him, the stronger her nervous buzz became.

"Here, I'll bring it in there for you. I've got it anyway."

"No, really, I can take it from here," she said to his back. She hurried behind him as he rolled the cart away from her, but stopped when Mrs. A laid a hand on her arm.

"Let him do it, dear. Men like to feel useful," said the older woman. "Besides," she added with a wink, "it's so nice to watch them work, isn't it?"

"Mrs. A!" Mandy shook her head, half laughing, half wincing. No one could ever accuse Madeline Arbuckle of being politically correct.

"Well, it's true. At my age, all I can do is look! But you, now, you can follow that very nice-looking young man into the library and have a lovely little chat before your meeting with the bride and groom. Who knows where that might lead?"

"Oh, please, Mrs. A! He's interested in my building, not in me."

"All the more reason you should go in there and have a friendly conversation. You catch more flies with honey than with vinegar, you know. And I don't think he knows it's your building yet," stated Mrs. A.

"Well, no, maybe not that I own it. But he knows where my business is, and I know he wants the building. We're kind of on opposite sides here."

"And you haven't heard the expression 'keep your friends close and your enemies closer'? So get in there, and get closer. And save me some leftover cake!"

Mandy shook her head, said good-bye, and headed into the Margaret Library. She found Kevin nose-deep in one of her binders of cake designs.

"See something you like?" she asked as she started to unload the cart.

"What? Oh, sorry." He put the binder down on the closest table. "Here, let me help. Those look heavy."

"No, that's okay. They're not heavy, but they are very carefully packed." She had two good-sized coolers, stuffed to the brim. Kevin picked up a trio of cardboard boxes, each the size of a large shoe box standing on end.

"What is all this?" He pointed with his chin, hands full of boxes.

"Samples for a wedding consultation. Want to put those over here?"

Mandy chose the big round table near the fireplace for her setup. It was big enough to display her cakes and fillings, and provided comfy overstuffed chairs for her clients. She liked this spot for wedding consultations. The old photograph of Margaret Thurston, the wife of the first owner of the hotel, taken on her wedding day in 1938, hung prominently over the fireplace. *Too bad Riley isn't using purple as one of her colors. The shade of the amethyst in Margaret's medallion would be lovely for flowers and linens in the ballroom upstairs.* As often as Mandy recommended it, so far none of her prospective brides had chosen that particular hue. *Oh, well, maybe I will, someday!*

She worked quickly, arranging and rearranging everything for maximum effect. Pleased with the results, she piled the empty containers onto the luggage cart and pushed it out of the way.

"All this for a consultation? Isn't this a little over the top?" Kevin asked. He leaned against the fireplace, leafing through her binder again.

"No, not really. Have you met the bride's mother?" Mandy laughed and shook her head. "Anyway, Riley has already confirmed I'll be doing the cake and desserts. This is to help her decide the cake and filling flavors. Which frosting I use will depend on the cake design, and we'll start working on that today too. Don't you make models sometimes, for the buildings you design?"

"Sure, but that's different."

"Why?"

"For one thing, no one consumes my models!" he retorted.

"True. So your models last past the end of your project. And then what? What will Harmony do with the model, or do you get it back? At least with mine, people actually do something with them!"

"Oh, really? You've got a lot of food here. I've seen Riley and her mother. I don't expect they'll actually eat all this," he said, waving his hand at the table, now covered with plates and platters and serving bowls. "This had to have cost a bunch. You said yourself, you already know you have the contract. Why go to all this effort?"

"Because it's good business. And none of it will go to waste. When I finish here, Mrs. A wants some of the leftovers, and I know which one is her favorite, so I'll drop some off with her. I deliver whatever's left in the store at the end of every day anyway to someplace that can use it, on a rotating schedule. Tonight's extras go to the hospital, for the ER and trauma nurses. I'll put any other cake slice leftovers in with their delivery."

"You do that every day?"

"When we can. We start fresh every morning. Some days we close early, if we run out. And some days we have leftovers to donate."

Kevin scratched his head. "How can that be a viable business model? Some days you don't have enough, and some days you have too much. Some days you stick to your posted hours, but some days you don't?"

"Welcome to the food service industry," Mandy replied, glancing down at her watch. "Look, unless there's something more you want to know, I need to finish getting ready." She turned and started walking for the door, hoping he would take the hint and follow.

As they walked out of the Margaret Library and into the lobby, he said, "One more question. If your business is successful enough you can afford to give away a lot of product regularly, then why are you here? Why haven't you moved to someplace like Calgary, someplace where you could expand, hire staff, maybe make enough to sell to restaurants?"

She stared at him in disbelief. "What makes you think I don't do any of those things now? Well, except for the moving to Calgary part. I have staff. I've expanded the kitchen out the back. And I have standing orders with the hotel here, with a couple of golf courses, and a couple more restaurants in town, for cakes and pies and other desserts."

"Seriously? Then why are you still here? Why limit yourself to this small town when your business could grow so much more in a place like Calgary?"

"Because some of us actually like living in a small town. Especially one like Harmony," she said, smiling with gritted teeth at Lilith Hamilton as she approached. It always paid to be on the good side of the mayor's wife, no matter how unpleasant she might be. Plus, Mandy really did prefer her small town and never hesitated to say so.

Riley rushed in behind her mother. "And we're so glad you do!" exclaimed the bride-to-be. "Who would do my wedding cake if Whimsy moved to Calgary? Hello, I'm Riley Hamilton. I think I've seen you around, haven't I?" she said, extending her hand to Kevin.

"Yes, I think so. You work at Anderson & Anderson, right? I've been in to talk to them about real estate holdings here in town." He shook her hand, then her mother's. "Mrs. Hamilton."

"Oh yes, you're the architect doing the town hall and community center, correct? My husband was very impressed with the design. And with your plans for revitalizing Main Street," said Lilith. "Goodness knows it could use a face-lift!"

Mandy caught Riley's eye-roll and turned away to hide a smile. Mrs. Hamilton's own "little nip and tuck" last year had been the talk of the town for days.

But Mandy knew Kevin planned more for Main Street than a minor face-lift: he proposed major surgery. "I hope we follow the same detailed approval process for this plan as we did for the town hall and community center. And I hope the council remembers their declared mandate for supporting local business, even if it means turning down big chains."

"Well, I'm sure little businesses like yours don't want the competition," replied Lilith. "But it's all about what's right for Harmony, isn't it? And you can be sure the men on council will have the best interests of the town at heart. Why, they—"

"Oh, Mother, you know there isn't a big chain bakery that could make a better wedding cake for me than Whimsy!" Riley linked her arm through her mother's and drew her toward the Margaret Library. "And that's why we're here today, isn't it? So we'll taste Mandy's wonderful samples, and I'll look at the pictures and dream about my wedding. Isn't that right, Mandy?"

"Of course." Mandy glanced back at Kevin as she followed the two women into the library. He stood in the hotel lobby, watching them. Watching her.

This whole encounter confused her. He hadn't been anything like she had expected, given their confrontation at the Chamber of Commerce meeting. That little buzz, there at the beginning? That was new. And a little weird. Nice, but weird.

She shook her head. As she turned back to her clients, she heard Brock Anderson, Riley's fiancé, greet Kevin on his way by. The two of them conversed in low tones, then Brock laughed and slapped Kevin on the back before ambling toward Mandy and the others as Kevin walked away.

"Am I late?" he asked, giving Riley a quick kiss and smiling at her mother.

"Not at all," declared Mandy. The grandfather clock chimed for four thirty as she ushered them over to her display. "Right on time. Riley, thank you for sending me the photos of your gown," she added as they all found seats.

"That gives me some ideas about cake design—or about cake decorating, I should say. First, let's talk about the flavors for the cakes and fillings. Then we can move on to frostings, and other decorations."

She carefully lifted the pretty china plate holding the first of her four cake samples. "I kept these undecorated and unfilled. Right now I want you to focus on the cake flavor itself. Here we have plain white vanilla cake, very traditional for weddings. The next one is—"

"No need to bring out any others. That's what we want," stated Lilith.

"Mom! We want to taste all of them, don't we, Brock? I asked Mandy for choices. I don't want a plain old vanilla cake. I want something... something more exciting! More fun! This is supposed to be the biggest party of my life. I want a fun cake to go with all the rest!"

Mandy reached for her cake knife and some serving plates as Riley and her mother argued about the flavor. Brock caught her eye. "Look, maybe we can get her to taste a couple? Maybe she'll be a little more... flexible?"

"We can try," Mandy replied.

She cut slices from each of the four samples. "Here, Mrs. Hamilton, why don't you try these? That first one, that's the plainest vanilla white cake. The next one"—she pointed as they tasted—"that's the champagne cake I used for January's cupcake of the month. It's a little moister, a little denser, but not quite as white."

"Oh, I like this one." Riley closed her eyes and savored the delicate taste of the second sample. "It's not as sweet either, is it?"

"Not quite. Moving to number three: I call this one eggnog cake. The cinnamon and nutmeg make you think of eggnog, although it's not as eggy. The spices make it a nice choice for a December wedding."

"Can we spike it with rum?" Brock grinned and held his plate out for another slice.

"On no account will there be rum in your wedding cake!" said Lilith with a disapproving sniff. "Even the champagne in the second one is questionable. You know your cousins from the US will be here. We need to show them a wedding in Canada can be elegant and refined, not a drunken free-for-all."

"I don't think there's enough champagne in a slice of cake to get anyone drunk, Mom."

"Be that as it may, I—"

Mandy headed off the argument with the last sample. "If you want a cake to celebrate Canada, how about this one? It's a maple ginger cake. Not white, but a firm, moist cake with a distinct maple taste."

"Oh, it's too hard to decide!" Riley said, moaning in pleasure at the new taste. "Brock, what do you think?"

"I think any of them would be a good choice, sweetheart. Whichever one you want is okay with me."

"There may be a way around having to choose. You said what, a hundred and fifty guests? This'll be a tiered cake, and you can have different flavors in different tiers. We'll give the wait staff the list and they can ask your guests which they prefer as the pieces are served."

"There, see, Mom? Now you can have the white cake you want, and I can have all the flavors I want." She wiggled in her chair. "What's next?"

"Fillings. Again, you can have a different one in each tier. Or you can use one throughout."

"Will the tiers have fillings? I figured they'd be layers of cake stacked up with frosting." Brock peered into the various bowls on the table.

Mandy took pity on him and started ladling fillings into custard cups, passing one of each to the three of them. "You could, but each tier can have two layers with filling between. That makes a nice high cake when you stack them up."

"Oh, man, that's good!" His eyes lit up as he tasted the samples. "What are all these?"

"You have a custard crème, kind of like an éclair filling. This one's raspberry, this one is lemon, that one is chocolate cream cheese, and the last one is peppermint," Mandy explained, pointing to each in turn. "We can also do a plainer cream cheese filling, maybe with a little lemon or orange. I'd have brought an almond cream cheese, or a ground walnut and brown sugar filling, but you said no nuts, right, Lilith? What do you think?"

"I still think you should have an all-white cake, Riley. Then if you wanted different fillings you could, I suppose.

Although I don't see why you would want to. It's so… casual. And untraditional."

Lilith might have complained about the cake choices, but Mandy noticed she ate every crumb of her four cake samples, and had started making inroads in the dollops of fillings in the little bowls in front of her.

"Do I have to decide today?" asked Riley.

"No, of course not," Mandy reassured her. "You can change your mind up to ten days before the wedding. If you can narrow it down before then, that's great too. And as for frostings: with the wedding gown picture you sent me, I'd recommend a fondant frosting, with beading and… well, here." She reached for her binders and opened the smaller of the two. "I put this together last night for you. Here's how I see the cake tiers with the fondant icing. See the beading and the tracery?"

"Oh, Mom, look! It matches my dress! Mandy, this is wonderful! Look, Brock, look at the detail!"

"And it's in your colors. Have you chosen which flowers yet? That version's got the roses, and if you turn the page…"

"Oh, look at the poinsettias! I really like it with the poinsettias. Even better than with the roses. But I'm still going back and forth between them and the roses for me and the bridesmaids to carry."

"Again, you can make the final decision later. And the flowers on the cake don't have to match your bouquet either.

You said you might decorate the room in poinsettias even if you carry roses. So the cake—"

"You're carrying roses, Riley, and that's final!" Lilith rose abruptly and faced her daughter. "I have put up with quite enough. You fought me on the dress, but you have to agree that this one," she declared, pointing to the photo on the front of the binder, "is by far the most beautiful. I will allow you some flexibility in the cake and fillings, because I know Mandy here is your friend and it's always good to support local businesses. But I will *not* have my daughter walk down the aisle to get married holding a... a potted plant!"

She grabbed her purse and coat from the back of her chair and stormed out, leaving dead silence in her wake.

Brock cleared his throat. "Well, that was fun."

Tears shimmered in Riley's eyes. "I don't want her mad at me. We have months to go yet before the wedding!"

"Oh, baby, don't cry," he said. He looked at Mandy as if to say *Help me!* with the typical male's panic at seeing a woman's tears. "We'll sort it out. She'll come around."

"But, but what if she doesn't? It's *my* wedding. I'm trying not to turn into Bridezilla here, but I want to have the wedding of *my* dreams, not hers!"

Mandy handed Riley a box of tissues. Years of dealing with stressed-out brides—and stress-inducing mothers of brides—had taught her to keep some handy for moments like these. "Brock, why don't Riley and I work through these choices and put together a plan? I really appreciate you coming today," she continued, standing and nudging him toward the door. "I love it when the groom takes an interest in the wedding day. We can talk about the rehearsal dinner desserts another time, if you want to be here for that appointment," she finished in a whisper as they reached the entrance.

"Up to Riley. I can show up again if she needs to finish planning another day." He looked back at his bride-to-be, who sniffled into a wad of tissues, her tears mostly stopped. "On the other hand, if you can finish up today... Tell Riley I'll grab a drink in the Peaks Bar and wait for her."

Chapter Four

The television over the bar played softly as the two patrons sitting at the far end stared raptly at a golf match. Kevin reached for a handful of pretzels and contemplated his options for dinner. He'd spent a lot of time in hotel bars, traveling as he did for his job. The Peaks Bar was nicer than most. The dark wood paneling shone with frequent polishing, the upholstered bar stools and the oversized captain's chairs, like the ones at his table, provided comfortable seating for a cozy evening, and the range of craft beers on tap was impressive for a small town.

He raised his draft and drank his first welcome swallow after a long day. Today had been a series of hassles, one after another, small but annoying, like mosquitoes trying to bite: you finished chasing one away and the next one tried to land. More irritants than real problems, but never-ending.

First the town engineer had complained about grading and drainage around the town hall for the new parking lot. Then the guys from Harmony Construction had, as usual, given him a hard time about his coffee. Why it should matter to them if he came back to his suite at the Thurston a couple of times a day to make himself coffee baffled him. So he didn't want to visit their favorite cupcake shop, so what? Harmony's downtown didn't have a Starbucks, for pity's sake! And it's not like he disappeared for hours on end. Not that his comings and goings should be any of their concern. Unlike them, he didn't punch an hourly time clock.

And when he finally finished for the day and came back to the hotel, his home away from home, who did he run into in the lobby? The owner of that very same cupcake shop. The very attractive owner, who turned out to be a whole lot more interesting than he had anticipated, based on their brief encounter at the Chamber of Commerce meeting.

She was smart, she was funny, she was cute as a button. She was, from all accounts, big hearted and active in the community on several fronts. And she owned a store in the building he wanted to tear down and replace.

How could he convince her to move? And if her cupcakes were as good as the HC guys said they were, why wasn't she itching to relocate to Calgary and make something more of herself? What kept her here in this little town?

Kevin shook his head and took another sip of his beer. He might never understand why she didn't want to move out of her old building. But it didn't matter. He'd come up with a plan to convince her otherwise, or work around her.

Maybe he'd have more success going directly to the building owner. He knew the building belonged to the Schmidt Family Corporation—but there were no more Schmidts in town, according to the phone book in his suite upstairs on the sixth floor.

And here came a potential source of information. He raised a hand as Brock Anderson stepped into the bar from the lobby. "Brock! Got a minute?"

Brock detoured to the bar to place an order before joining Kevin at his little table in the corner. "I've got plenty of minutes. Riley's finishing up with Mandy, and I told her I'd wait for her in here. I need a beer."

"Wedding planning getting under your skin?" Kevin said with a laugh.

"Not the wedding plans. Those are going great. Riley's great. But my future mother-in-law can be a real pain, you know?" Brock shook his head, a rueful expression on his face. He accepted his beer from the server and took a grateful sip.

"I've only met her a couple of times," Kevin said. "I'm glad I deal with the mayor and not his wife." That was as much as he'd say out loud. Never a good idea to bad-mouth the wife of the mayor, when you wanted to make something happen in a community, even if he did find her unpleasant and interfering.

Brock chuckled. "It's a good thing Ed's such a great guy, and I am very glad Riley takes after her dad and not her mother."

"I hear ya. So… what's the deal with the wedding cake? How did you two choose a cupcake maker to do a wedding cake? Won't that be a bit of a stretch for her?"

"Have you tasted her stuff? No, that's right, you won't go there for coffee with the rest of the guys," teased Brock.

Kevin sputtered on his beer. "How does everybody know that? And why does anybody care?"

"Hey, it's a small town. Everybody knows everybody's business here."

"So I've noticed. So, then, can you tell me who owns the Schmidt building?"

"Nope. Can't. No, really, it's privileged. The corporation's a client"—the lawyer shrugged—"and they've asked not to reveal the owners. I can pass on a message, but that's about it."

"Can you set up a meeting?"

"I can ask, sure. This is about buying the land and the building, right? I doubt they'll be interested in hearing a sales pitch. The Schmidt family used to own a whole lot more along Main Street. They've held on to the last chunk, and I can't see them wanting to sell now."

"They'd be well paid. I have a pool of investors interested in Harmony. There are some other commercial properties we're looking at, too, and maybe a residential neighborhood."

Brock sipped his beer. "It's not the money. The building is a family legacy. It's all that's left from the original holdings. You know these small towns. Their community pride sometimes outweighs their common sense."

"Tell me about it." Kevin shook his head. "I don't get it. Take your cupcake girl. Everybody says how great her cupcakes are, or her weddings cakes," he said, nodding at Brock, "and how successful her business is. So why wouldn't she be interested in moving to Calgary, opening a bigger place?"

Brock shrugged. "Not everyone wants to move to the big city. There's a lot to be said for small-town life."

"Yeah? What? I grew up outside of a town like this, on a farm. I couldn't wait to get out of there. Even my folks have sold out and moved to Arizona."

"I don't know. I kind of like living here. I had to be talked into it at first, but then Riley said yes, and she didn't want to move, and my uncle made me a partner, so…"

"So you're staying. Any regrets about leaving the big city?"

Brock laughed at him. "It's not like we're far away! It's, what, barely over an hour's drive? We go often enough. There's some stuff you can't get here. But you know what? We're going less and less often. I expect once we start having kids, our lives will really be rooted here."

"You say you can't get everything here. Wouldn't it make living in Harmony easier if you could?"

"You mean, if we had the big chains like Home Depot here? Or Starbucks?" Brock asked. "Might mean a little less driving, and be a little more convenient, sure, but I'm not convinced it would be better. And getting in the big chains will be an uphill battle. A lot of established businesses here don't want them in. Hell, a lot of the residents don't want them in."

"Oh, sure, the older folks. I can see that. But—"

"Not only the older folks. Take the young families. They like living here; it's a better place to raise kids. Cleaner, safer, quieter: there's a list. We've got great affordable housing.

And decent schools. And community activities, for kids and adults. Those tourism dollars go a long way to paying for services for the locals."

"Should I count you as one of the opposition?" Kevin asked, only half joking.

"Maybe more neutral than opposed. At least at this point. And that's me, personally, as a resident. As a lawyer, I have to tell you Anderson & Anderson represents quite a few businesses in town. Many of them will be strongly opposed."

"Like your cupcake girl."

"She's not my girl. I've got a girl of my own, thanks." Brock looked at Kevin appraisingly. "Maybe she could be your cupcake girl."

"What, win her over and then buy her out?"

"The buying out? Maybe not so much. The winning over? Maybe. Who knows? She's not seeing anyone at the moment. She and Riley are friends; they go back to when they were kids." He rocked his glass back and forth on the coaster. "Did you know she's got an item up for bid in the silent auction?"

At Kevin's blank look, Brock continued, "The fundraiser for the new playground? Mentioned at the Chamber of Commerce meeting? Mandy entered a fancy dinner for two, to be prepared at the winner's home. The value is listed at $250, I think. If you were to place a really big bid, you'd make some points and impress the girl."

"Not a bad idea," mused Kevin. "And if I made her the guest, she'd be making a fancy dinner for the two of us. I'd have her undivided attention for the whole evening." He looked at Brock. "Don't tell your fiancée, okay? I don't want cupcake girl to find out."

"No worries. And on that note…" He raised his glass and drank down the last of his beer. "Here comes my girl. Looks like she's calmed down, which means I'll have a better evening."

Riley wove through the tables to their corner. Brock stood and kissed her lightly. "All set?"

"I hope so. Mandy and I settled a lot of the details, and we'll do the rest as soon as I can figure out how to get Mom to agree," Riley replied.

"Don't sweat it, hon. Tell your dad what you want and he'll make sure you get it."

Riley giggled. "I'm keeping my dad as my last resort. I don't want to play the favorite-daughter card too often or it loses some of its punch. Anyway, are you ready to go?"

"Sure." As he helped her on with her coat, he said, "Nice seeing you, Kevin. And good luck!"

Chapter Five

"**M**andy! Phone for you!"

"Oh, thanks, Zak." Mandy dried her hands on the towel draped over her shoulder and took the handset. "This is Mandy Brighton of Whimsy, how can I help you?"

"Hey, Mandy, it's Wendy Thurston. I wanted to give you a heads-up before you start getting calls congratulating you."

"Congratulating me? What for?" Mandy wandered over to where Kelsey was tinting a batch of gum paste and nodded her approval at the delicate pink. They were scheduled to spend the evening making dozens of candy roses to decorate a wedding cake for the coming weekend, colored to match the bridesmaids' dresses.

"For bringing in the single largest bid in the silent auction. Who knew someone would bid five thousand dollars for a dinner valued at two hundred and fifty?" Wendy laughed when Mandy gasped.

"What? That can't be right. You sure you haven't added a zero in there? There's no way anyone in Harmony would bid so much!"

"Maybe it wasn't anyone from Harmony…"

"Who else could it be? Out-of-towners and tourists wouldn't even know about it, would they?" Mandy pulled out a stool and sat at the big central worktable. "What have you heard? How come you know about this? I thought the bids were anonymous."

"They are. That's why I don't know who placed it, not officially. Katherine will start contacting the high bidders as soon as she gets here. She asked me to pull the bid sheets down from the bulletin board, which is when I noticed the high one on yours! Anyway," she finished, "I wanted to warn you to start expecting some calls. I don't want to tie up your phone line—bye!"

"Thanks, I think?" Mandy pulled the handset from her ear, gave it a puzzled look as she disconnected, and returned it to Zak.

"Who was on the phone?" Kelsey set the first bowl aside, reached for the next one and more food coloring, and started on the batch of deeper pink.

"Wendy. Chamber secretary. Wanted to tell me my little dinner has for some reason pulled in this outrageously high bid, and warn me I should start expecting more calls about it." She shook her head. "I will never understand people."

"Who's the big spender? Anybody we know?"

"I don't know. Wendy didn't know either. Everyone filled out their bids with bidding numbers, not their names. Katherine kept the master list a secret." Mandy pulled over a bowl and sat down to tint the green gum paste they'd use for the leaves.

"How much did they bid? Must have been a whopper to get her all excited!"

"Five grand."

Kelsey's bowl hit the counter with a thump. "*How* much? She's kidding, right?"

"Don't think so. I wish I knew who made the bid."

Mandy measured out the green coloring as the phone rang again. "And so it continues…"

Zak brought the phone in again and she reached to take it. Out of the corner of her eye, she saw Kelsey mouth *Katherine?* and Zak shake his head and whisper back, "No, the mayor."

"Hello, this is Mandy… Yes, Ed, hello. I did hear from Wendy. You were outbid?" She rolled her eyes at her friends and flapped her free hand like a puppet talking.

She bit her lip to keep from laughing as Zak strutted around her kitchen, pretending to shake hands with the various appliances. Ed had done a lot of glad-handing around town during the last election, and apparently Zak had been less than impressed. "Yes, sir, I'll do the town proud. So you don't know… Yes, it'll be a dinner to remember. I'll look forward to hearing from Katherine." She hung up and handed the phone to Zak again.

"Best get out front, Zak," prompted Kelsey. "When word of this gets out, the place will be packed!"

Mandy waited impatiently for the phone to ring again as the two of them returned to their tasks. She hopped up and off her stool and made it halfway to the door by the second ring.

"Hello, this is Mandy Brighton of... Oh, hi, Dory. I expected Katherine... Yes, I heard it from Wendy. And then Ed called. No, I still don't know who the high bidder is. Please don't tell me the ladies at the Clip and Curl are taking bets on who placed the high bid!"

She dropped onto her stool and rested her elbows on the stainless steel work surface. Pinching the bridge of her nose with her free hand, she squeezed her eyes shut as she listened to the caller. Kelsey had both hands over her mouth to stifle her own laughter.

"What's so... funny?" Suzette's voice dropped to a whisper as Kelsey hushed her and pointed to Mandy on the phone. "Really, what's so funny?" she said more quietly.

Kelsey shook her head. Together they watched Mandy finish up the call, set down the receiver, and drop her head to her hands. "Oh, no. It keeps getting better."

"What are the bets? Who's in the lead?" Kelsey prompted.

"Well," Mandy said, raising her head, "the front runner at one point was Ed Hamilton, but he told me it wasn't him. Next in line was the wife of the guy who owns the steak house, because Dory says she's been in at the Clip and Curl getting her hair done a lot and she—the wife, not Dory—says her marriage has lost its sparkle and that she likes to do things to shake up her husband. Betting five grand on a dinner worth two fifty is sure going to do that!"

"Nah, won't be her. It'll be a guy. You think it's our friendly sleazebucket from the Chevy dealer?"

"Eeeew." Suzette gave an exaggerated shudder. "I hope not. He gives me the creeps. I wouldn't want to have to go to his house and cook dinner."

"Oh, oh, oh, I know!" exclaimed Kelsey. "It's—"

"Hold that thought," Mandy said as the phone rang one more time. "Hello, this is Mandy Brighton of... Hello, Katherine. Yes, I've been expecting your call. Seems like half the town knows about the bid, but not who placed it. I understand why you wanted to contact the successful bidders before talking to the people who provided the prizes... So, who is it?"

The blood left her face in a rush, and the worry settled into her stomach like a hot ball of lead. She must have swayed where she sat; Suzette came behind and put a steadying hand on her shoulder.

Swallowing hard, Mandy finished up the call. "Well. Not what I expected. Thanks for letting me know. He'll give me a call to set it up? Okay, I'll expect to hear from him in a couple of days, I guess. Thanks."

"Well? Don't keep us in suspense! Who is it? You know we love you, Mandy, and you're going to make a kick-ass dinner. But who would bid so much?" Kelsey listened intently from the other side of the table.

Mandy swallowed again. The words were hard to get out around her tight throat. "It's the new guy, Kevin MacNeal. You know, the architect?"

"Shut up!" Three voices sounded as one before they broke into separate babbles.

"No way!"

"But he goes out of his way to avoid you!"

"What's his angle?"

The last one came through loud and clear. "Angle? What do you mean, angle?" Suzette asked Kelsey, who vibrated from excitement.

"I'll tell you what his angle is! Somehow he's going to use your catered dinner in his… his battle to get you to sell the building. Maybe he'll complain after, and make it sound like you did a terrible job, which we of course all know will *not be true*! But maybe he'll try to ruin your reputation, or at least make it harder for you to expand into a café next door. Or maybe," Kelsey enthused, "maybe he thinks he'll seduce you after dinner and try to change your mind about staying in Harmony and get you to go back to Calgary with him!"

Mandy stared at her friend, her mind a blank. *Where is this coming from?* "Kelsey, you know I love you, but you are certifiably nuts."

"No, wait, hear me out! This is supposed to be a romantic dinner, right? Isn't that how you described it on the bid sheet? And he's alone here, he's not dating anyone in town, at least not as far as I know. And Mrs. A says he's attracted to you, even though he never comes in here so I don't know how that happened. And—"

"Wait, wait, wait. You talked about him with Mrs. A? When did you do that? *Why* did you do that? And she's only ever seen us together once, at Riley's cake tasting. He's not attracted to me, he's annoyed with me."

48

Kelsey shook her head. "Denial, all I hear is denial. At least admit you're attracted to him! And, now that I think of it…"

"Be afraid, be very afraid," Zak whispered to Mandy. "It's always scary when she thinks."

"Shut up, Zak, and help me plan. You can turn this thing around. Instead of him seducing you and getting you to fall in love with him and changing your mind about selling the building and leaving Harmony, *you* seduce *him*! Make him fall in love with you, and he'll give up on any plans to buy you out and shut you down."

Mandy stared at her friends. "I should have entered a fancy cake, not a whole dinner. Then this wouldn't be happening."

"No, I like it," stated Suzette. "She's right, you can make this work for you, if you get back control of the situation."

"Get back control? I never had it in the first place! And what—"

"So take control. From the beginning. Let him think he's setting you up, and then you take him down," Kelsey said firmly.

Mandy shook her head. "I've got a very bad feeling about this…"

Chapter Six

Kevin forced the door closed, though not quite fast enough to prevent the cold March wind from following him inside the office of Anderson & Anderson. The sudden breeze ruffled his hair, then continued past him to stir the top papers on the receptionist's desk. He nodded at Riley Hamilton as she yanked over her metal nameplate and slammed it down on the loose pages before they could blow away.

She held up her finger and mouthed *One minute* before returning to her phone call. "Gotta go, Dad. I wanted to thank you for getting Mother to back down about the wedding cake. By the time I got home last night, she was almost calm enough to hear what Mandy and I came up with… No, I haven't finalized everything with her but we can finish later. Yes, I'll let you know how much the deposit will be and when it's due. Love you, Dad!"

Riley hung up and gave Kevin a weary smile. "You're here to see Brock?" At his nod, she continued, "He's finishing up with his four thirty appointment. Have a seat and he'll be right with you. And I apologize for being on the phone. My mother made things difficult at our cake tasting yesterday," she said, pressing one finger against her temple and rubbing hard.

Kevin took the comfy chair closest to her desk. "So I understand. Wouldn't it have been easier to get a cake made by someone in Calgary?"

"My mother wanted to. But no one makes wedding cakes better than Mandy's. Hers actually taste as good as they look!" she said, laughing. "But you're not here to listen to my cake issues."

"No, but I'm trying to understand your friend a little better. If she's so good, she could be a lot bigger in a place like Calgary. Why does she stay here, in such an old building?"

"You mean, besides the fact her family has run the best bakery in town in that very spot since before the Thurston Hotel opened? And the only relative she cares about lives here in Harmony?"

"She has relatives here?" he asked casually.

"Oh, sure! When Mandy came back to Harmony, she bought out her great-aunt after her great-uncle died, and turned the family bakery into Whimsy. Mandy moved into the apartment above the store, and Anna moved into the Residence at Pineview. She still lives there. She pals around with Emily Jamieson—you know, who used to be Emily Thurston and who ran the hotel till she retired?—and Madeline Arbuckle. The three of them are something when they get on a tear!" Riley laughed.

"I can imagine." Kevin chuckled, shaking his head. "I've met Mrs. Arbuckle."

"Oh, right, you're staying in one of the Thurston suites, aren't you? You probably see her almost every day. You may have seen Mandy's great-aunt too."

"Maybe. So tell me more about Mandy and her great-aunt. You called her the only relative Mandy cares about. What about her parents?"

"I don't know anything about her father. I'm not sure anyone does, including Mandy. But her mother…? Not my favorite person. I don't want to come off like the village gossip, though. If you want to know more, you should ask Mandy herself." Riley shook her head as she rose from her chair and headed toward the office door opening down the hall. "It looks like Brock's about ready for you. Here comes his last appointment."

Brock walked his client to the front door and shook the older man's hand. "And congratulations again on your new grandson. I'll call you when the papers are ready to sign."

He turned to Kevin. "Hey, good to see you, man. Come on back."

Kevin followed him into his office as Brock continued, "I heard you won Mandy's silent auction prize. Are you interested in our cupcake girl?"

"I'm interested in her building, certainly. I wanted to ask you if you'd had a chance to talk to the owners about selling." Kevin settled into the leather wingback chair in front of the big oak desk and looked around the room. "Nice office. Times must be good in small-town Alberta."

"Not if you've been working in the oilfield. But I can't complain. Despite the downturn in the Alberta economy, Uncle Reg made it worth my while to relocate here. I sure wouldn't have made partner in my dad's firm anytime soon."

Brock leaned his chair back and swung it gently from side to side. "So. The Schmidt building. You know it's owned by a privately held family corporation, right?"

"Yeah, so you told me. What I want is information on the owners. There aren't any more Schmidts in Harmony. Or none I can find, anyway."

"No, there aren't," agreed Brock. "You could pull the corporate registry, you know."

"Sure. But as people keep reminding me, this is a small town. Everyone knows everyone else's business. What's the scoop on the owners of the building? Why so secretive?"

"Not so much secretive as private. The family has had some... internal problems, I guess you'd call them. I can't get into details; they don't want me airing their dirty laundry."

"I get that," Kevin stated. "But privacy concerns shouldn't have anything to do with selling the building, should it?"

"Well, no, maybe not. But the building is the last bit of real estate in the corporation, and they want to hang on to it. And don't be so skeptical," the lawyer said. "It's profitable. Very much so. All four commercial bays are leased, and one of the apartments. The other three cycle through seasonal tenants."

"Rumor has it the owner of the yarn shop wants to retire."

"And your girl Mandy intends to expand into the space," Brock shot back. "It'll be empty only long enough for her to renovate it into a café and kitchen."

Kevin sighed. "Again, she's not my girl. And you think her plan is feasible? How can the owner of a cupcake store in Harmony be doing well enough to afford such a big expansion?"

"Look, Kevin, I know you want the building. I don't think you'll get it. Mandy has a strong business plan, and the financial chops to implement it. The town loves her—not only her baking, but the woman herself. That bakery has been in her family for generations. It's a town landmark. No chain store you can name could replace it."

"But—"

"I really can't tell you any more. If you want to understand her and her business, talk to Mandy herself! Isn't that why you made such an outrageous bid on her silent auction entry?" teased Brock.

"Says the man who suggested I do it."

"Not for five grand, I didn't!"

"Heard about that, did you?"

"Everyone has heard about it by now! If you're surprised, you seriously underestimated the power and speed of small-town chatter. Social media has nothing on how news goes viral in Harmony," he warned, laughing. "So, take notice: whatever you do with your cupcake girl is going to be the talk of the town by the next day."

"She's not my cupcake girl! Why do you keep saying that?" Kevin rolled his eyes as he stood to leave.

"Because even though you've never set foot in her shop, you've shown more interest in her than the guys who go in there every day for cupcakes and coffee. Maybe you should think about rectifying the situation."

"What, showing interest? It's the building I want, not the girl!"

"Yeah, you keep saying that. But I meant you should rectify not visiting the shop and having one of her cupcakes. This month it's Lucky Shamrock cupcakes." Brock rolled his eyes and smacked his lips. "Had one after lunch. Outstanding."

"What do you mean, this month?" Kevin asked as they left the office and walked down the hall.

"Oh, she's got monthly specials, a different cupcake of the month. There's always the standards, and they're great, but the featured ones? Amazing. Riley and I are considering some of those cakes and frostings for our wedding cake layers. Right, hon?" he said as they reached Riley's desk in reception.

"And they were so good at the tasting yesterday! I think we even had one she hasn't featured yet. It's going to be so much fun to see what she comes up with for the design, for four different layers!" Riley enthused. "I've still got one of this month's specials left from this morning—want to try it?"

"Hey, you told me they were all gone!" protested her fiancé.

"I'm saving you from yourself. You didn't need two. And anyway, these are supposed to be for clients. Here, Kevin," she said, holding out the box, "try this."

Kevin eyed the offering. The shiny white bakery box said "Whimsy: Cupcakes, Celebration Cakes, and Specialty Desserts" and an address and phone number in bright green, next to a hand-drawn cupcake, yellow with pink frosting. Inside the box sat a single cupcake: white with pale-green frosting and deep-green (gumdrop?) shamrocks nestled on top, the whole thing cupped in white paper branded with the Whimsy logo.

The scents of peppermint and vanilla tickled his nose as he reached for it, mouth watering. Sweets weren't usually his thing unless chocolate or maple syrup was involved, but he had to admit it looked and smelled amazing.

"Humph. You should have made him go get one himself, so he'd go see the store," Brock complained. He reached into the box and swiped his finger through some frosting stuck to the inside.

"Oh, I don't think that'll be a problem." Riley laughed and pointed. "Look at his face. He won't be able to stop at one!"

"Wow. This is great," Kevin said after swallowing the first bite.

"See? Told you! Now, go check out Whimsy and see what else Mandy has today."

"And you should talk to her about your dinner too," added Brock, escorting Kevin to the door. "Set it up for pretty soon, maybe this weekend? That way—"

"Wait, you won the bid for Mandy's dinner? Does she know yet?" Riley interjected.

"Probably," replied Kevin. "It sounds like everyone else does!"

"Oh, wow! I have to talk to her. Are you going over there now? I'll let her know you're coming." She reached for the phone.

Kevin winced. "Maybe later. Or tomorrow."

"No, go now!" Riley glanced at the clock on the wall. "It's past the after-school rush but before the get-dessert-for-dinner rush. She'll have time to talk to you now."

His phone rang, and he glanced down at the screen. "Sorry, Riley, I have to take this. It'll probably take the rest of the afternoon to sort out. So I'll drop by... maybe tomorrow?"

"See that you do!"

Riley's voice rang in Kevin's ear as he made a quick exit and stepped outside the building. The town engineer's voice came through his cell, with another complaint about rainwater runoff from the construction site. He quickly explained to the man that with the rough grading scheduled for next week, any drainage issues would be fixed then.

He finished the call and then the cupcake—admittedly delicious—and tossed the crumpled paper into a trash can at the corner. He crossed Main Street and walked along the side of the Thurston Hotel to its front entrance, thinking hard.

Brock had been less forthcoming than he had hoped. He still didn't know who owned Mandy's building.

But now he had an in: the bid that won him a fancy catered dinner. Not only should the amount of the bid impress the girl, but she'd be his captive audience for the evening. He'd be able to talk her around, he was sure.

Now all he had to do was make certain she didn't back out of the dinner once she found out what he was planning.

Chapter Seven

The heavy double doors at the Thurston Hotel didn't block the damp March wind any better than the single one at Anderson & Anderson had. Kevin rubbed his cold hands together briskly before unbuttoning his coat in the welcome warmth. He glanced back out into the clear wintry evening. It didn't look like snow, but it had sure felt like it on his walk back from the job site.

The noise in the main lobby rose steadily as he approached the Peaks Bar. It reached an uncomfortable level when he stuck his head around the corner and looked in. Apparently the rerun of last night's hockey game had brought in the local crowd, who were hotly contending a penalty call. Again. From the sounds of it, most of them had seen the game last night.

He shook his head and continued down the lobby. *Small towns. Nothing better to do than watch hockey reruns.* He'd grab a drink in the Thomas Lounge before dinner—he needed one after being cooped up in his construction trailer with the town engineer for the last couple of hours—and plan his next move in getting hold of the prime piece of real estate he coveted.

The bartender looked up from mixing a drink, and waved at Kevin to find his own seat. He headed for a table away from the door when he heard his name being called.

"Mr. MacNeal! How lovely to run into you again. Do join me for a drink, won't you?" Madeline Arbuckle called from where she sat enthroned in an overstuffed armchair close to the fireplace.

Seating himself in the matching chair on the other side, he ordered a beer from the server who had followed him to the table. "Thank you, Mrs. Arbuckle. What brings you in here tonight?"

"Oh, I pop in every night after dinner for a little something to help me sleep." She raised her almost-empty glass to the server. "Another vodka and tonic, please. With an extra lemon slice."

Drinks ordered, she turned to Kevin. "So what brings you in here? Not interested in dissecting the hockey game in the bar?"

"Not so much. I like a good game as much as anybody, but once you've seen a match there's not much point in watching the rerun." He shrugged. "And it's too noisy in there to think."

"Oh, thinking, is it? That sounds terribly serious. What cause does a fine young man like yourself have for spending his evening thinking? Shouldn't you be out socializing?"

Kevin couldn't believe his ears. Was she flirting with him? Oh, man, he hoped not! Suppressing a shudder, he replied, "I don't know a lot of people in town. The nightlife here is, well, a little limited when you don't know anyone. And I'm here to work, really, so…"

"Nonsense. No one can work all the time. As for our nightlife being limited, it's true we don't have the same range of experiences you might find in Calgary. I guess that's why we make our own fun. Speaking of fun," she said, finishing up her drink as the server brought the new ones, "I hear you placed the highest bid on the fancy dinner our very own Mandy Brighton entered in the silent auction."

"How does everyone know already? I didn't think the auction results had been announced publicly yet!"

"Oh, I have my ways," she said with a smile. "And while the official announcement comes this weekend, at the dance, well, you were notified, weren't you? And so was Mandy, which means her employees know, among others. I heard it from my good friend, Anna Lipiczki. She's Mandy's great-aunt, although Mandy just calls her Auntie Anna, you know."

He murmured his assent, and she continued, "And she's so proud of the girl! Why, no one could have foreseen changing the store from a regular bakery to a cupcake and desserts bakery would be so successful, could they?"

"It used to be a different kind of bakery? I had heard it had a new name, since she took over, but I didn't know she changed the format too."

"Oh, my, yes! Mandy's family has run a bakery in that spot for generations. Her great-great-grandfather Karl, Anna's grandfather, started the Schmidt Bakery in 1914. Why, that's even before the Thurston Hotel opened!" Mrs. A sat back, pleased at having imparted something he obviously didn't know.

"Wait. Her great-grandfather was Karl Schmidt? And he owned the building, and the lot it sits on?"

"Great-great-grandfather, not great-grandfather," Madeline corrected. "And yes. That land has been in their family for generations, as has the building and the bakery. It's a real piece of Harmony history."

"The Schmidt family. Yes, I know. I found out that much when I started looking at the property. It's still owned by the Schmidt Family Corporation. But there are no more Schmidts, are there?"

"No one with the name, anyway. Anna and Mandy are the only direct descendants still in Harmony. Anna's sister Katya, Mandy's grandmother, lives in Calgary with her husband." She wrinkled her nose in distaste. "Unpleasant people, the pair of them. They washed their hands of their only daughter when she had Mandy, and they've never done a thing for our girl. Why, they didn't even give her a place to stay when she went to pastry school!"

"They don't have anything to do with the family holdings? It's only Mandy and her great-aunt?"

"That's right," Madeline confirmed. "Katya married some fancy businessman from Calgary and moved away. Anna stayed here and married Joe Lipiczki. They both worked in the bakery and took it over when Kurt died. When Katya and her husband William threw out their daughter, Janine came here and had the baby. Anna and Joe took them in out of the goodness of their hearts. They never had children themselves, and oh, they loved Janine's little girl! It used to break their hearts when Janine would run off and take Mandy with her."

"Mandy didn't grow up here? I thought she went to school with Riley Hamilton, the mayor's daughter."

"She did, when she stayed here. Janine would drag her away for months at a time, but she always brought Mandy back when she got tired of playing mommy. And when Mandy turned eighteen she chose to leave her mother. She finished up high school here, and then stayed here for good. Well, except for when she went away for pastry chef training, of course." Madeline smiled at him over the rim of her glass. "I take it this means you're interested in our girl?"

Kevin thought fast. His primary focus was her property, especially now he knew she co-owned it. What could it hurt to let the town think he also wanted the owner?

But how to get around her, since she had been so opposed to the development idea at the Chamber meeting? Maybe he could use this pretended interest as a smoke screen, and go after the property a different way.

"Since I entered the winning bid on her fancy dinner, I thought I'd get to know her a little bit before I collect. I didn't know about her family history. It's always interesting to know more about the people you see every day, don't you think?"

His explanation satisfied Madeline Arbuckle. For the next hour she regaled him with stories: about the town, about the history, about the people.

Eventually, after another vodka tonic, she wound down. "Oh, my, look at the time! I must get upstairs and watch my show. Walter and I watch *Jeopardy* every evening. He says it's the only thing worth watching besides the news." She creaked a little as she rose from her chair, but looked stable enough once she was on her feet.

Kevin stood when she did, and watched her walk slowly but steadily to the door. She paused to say something to their server, making the girl laugh.

Jason, the bartender, came over to clear the glasses. "Can I get you another beer?"

Kevin shook his head, and asked him who Walter was. "I thought her little dog was Betty Jo or Betty Jean or something."

"The dog is Betty Jo, although Gill calls her Killer. Walter Arbuckle was Mrs. A's husband. Died about five years ago now. She talks to the air sometimes as if he's still there next to her!" Jason laughed and shook his head. "Some of the more gullible staff claim they hear him moving around in the hotel at night, or smell his pipe."

"And it doesn't bother you, hearing this place might be haunted?"

"Nah." Jason took the empties up to the bar, and Kevin followed. "I don't believe in the woo-woo stuff. I've never heard or seen or smelled anything myself. But if it makes Mrs. A happy, what's the harm?"

"Uh huh. So tell me," Kevin changed the subject, "about Mandy Brighton and her family. And her business. She supplies to the restaurant here, right?"

"Sure. Chef Guy does okay with pastries and desserts, but he'd rather get them from her. Frees him up to be more creative on the main courses, he says. If he could get her to do bread as well as desserts I think he'd be in heaven." Jason looked at him curiously. "Why so interested in our girl, then?"

"It's no secret I want to develop the property Whimsy rents. I figure anything I can find out about Mandy Brighton and her business can only help."

"Maybe," the bartender said as he stowed the dirty glasses in the dishwasher under the counter. "You're going to get some resistance from a lot of folks here. There's history in that building, as much as in this one. Family businesses are important in small towns, more than in a big city like Calgary. We take care of our own."

"So I've learned. What I'd like to talk to her about is opportunities she might have in those big cities she doesn't have here."

"Then you'd best start with her great-aunt. As long as Anna Lipiczki is here, Mandy isn't going to be in any hurry to leave. And good luck getting Anna to change her mind. Her grandfather started the bakery in 1914, then her father ran it for years. Her husband is buried here. She's not likely to go live somewhere else at this point."

"But will she stand in Mandy's way?"

Chapter Eight

Mandy's head popped up from where she was refilling the insulated bottle of cream at one of the coffee stations. "Hi, Auntie Anna! I'll be with you in a minute," she said. "Zak, could you—"

"Of course!" Zak hurried from behind the counter to the front of the shop. "Hello, Mrs. Lipiczki, let me get that for you," he said, holding the door for her. "Look at that yellow! You've brought a ray of sunshine in here on such a gray day."

Standing on the threshold, Anna turned around and carefully shook off her bright umbrella before folding it closed and leaning it in the wicker basket Whimsy used as an umbrella stand. "It doesn't feel much like spring today, so I brought my spring with me," she declared. "Be a dear and bring me one of Mandy's salted caramel swirl cupcakes, would you? And a large coffee?"

"What, you don't want a Lucky Shamrock cupcake?" Mandy asked, wiping her hands on the towel she kept tucked at her waist.

"Not this early in the day, I don't think. Besides, no matter what cupcake of the month you feature, I think your salted caramel swirl is still my favorite." Anna took off her coat and brushed off some of the wetness before walking to the table farthest from the door. "Thank you for making some time for me this afternoon, my dear."

"Of course. I always have time for you! Let me grab a coffee too."

Mandy passed Zak as he delivered the order. At his raised eyebrows, she gave a little shrug. No, she didn't know why her great-aunt had called earlier to say she intended to stop by. Auntie Anna popped in once or twice a week, usually in the morning, to sit by the big sunny window and chat with anyone who came in. She didn't usually call ahead to make sure her great-niece was free.

By the time Mandy returned with her own coffee, the two were laughing over some story. Zak stood up when Mandy pulled out a chair. "Mrs. L, you're killing me here," he said, rolling his eyes as he left them to chat.

Mandy sat and picked up her coffee. "Okay, Auntie Anna, what's up?"

"Do I need an excuse to visit my favorite grand-niece and have my favorite cupcake at my favorite cupcake shop?"

"No, but you don't usually call ahead and make an appointment either. What gives?"

"I was thinking about when you finished your pastry chef training. You came back to Harmony and took over the bakery. You didn't have to," Anna said.

"Of course I did. What else should I have done: moved away and left you here alone?" Mandy shook her head. "Harmony is the only place I've ever felt I belonged. You and Uncle Joe gave me the only real home I ever had."

"Oh, sweetheart, you know you always had a home with us! I wish your mother could have settled down and stayed here. It would have been good for her, and for you, growing up, if she'd stayed in one place."

"Maybe, but it's water under the bridge. She didn't want to stay, and she sure didn't want to work in the bakery. She didn't want to work at all. Better for you and Uncle Joe to have paid out her inheritance years ago than to have her try to get something from the family business now," Mandy retorted. "I'm glad Whimsy was always separate. There's no way she can try to get anything out of my company!"

"Now, Mandy, she's still your mother. Would you really not help her?"

"I might be convinced to help pay for rehab, if she asked, and I thought there might be a chance she meant it this time. But there's no way I'd give her money. She got a good settlement when you bought her out. If she's run through it already, then she'd run through anything I gave her now." Mandy shook her head. "But you didn't come here to talk about my mother and money. What's up?"

"Not about your mother, not directly. But it is about money," Anna replied. "And about you. Are you happy here?"

"Of course I'm happy here! Why wouldn't I be? I've got you, and my friends, and a great business. I love this town. I love how people take care of each other. I love the history, the community, how close we are to the mountains and to Calgary." Running out of steam, she sipped her coffee. "What brought this on?"

"I ran into Brock Anderson at Bob's Grocery this morning and he asked me to pop by his office after I took my groceries home. When I got there, he asked me if the corporation would consider selling our land on Main Street. He said there's someone interested in buying, someone with a pool of investors. So I thought, if you were ever thinking about selling and moving to someplace like Calgary, this would be a good time."

"Uh huh. And did he happen to mention who this buyer is?"

"We didn't get that far. I said I would talk to you first."

"And now you've talked to me. And I'm not interested in selling," Mandy replied. She looked intently at her great-aunt, wanting to see her reaction. "Unless you are? Auntie Anna, do you want to sell your half of the corporation? I'll buy you out, even if I have to take a mortgage on the property to do it."

"Oh, no! Don't do that!" Auntie Anna's eyes widened in dismay. "We own the land and the building free and clear. There hasn't been a mortgage on this property since before I was born! I won't have you go into debt over this!"

Mandy shrugged. "It's not like I couldn't pay it back. We make enough in rents to cover a mortgage. And Whimsy is doing well. I might have to delay my expansion—"

"Stop right there, young lady! I won't hear of it! I don't need you to buy me out. I have plenty to live on, from when you bought me out of the bakery and turned it into Whimsy, plus what I get from the rentals. No more talk of mortgages and loans."

"Then no more talk about selling, all right?" She smiled at her great-aunt and stood, relieved to have straightened things out. "I need to get back to work. We're good?"

"We're good."

Mandy kissed Anna on the cheek and headed back into the kitchen. On her way past the register, Zak asked, "What was that all about?"

"Our lawyer wanted to meet with Auntie Anna about selling the land. Don't worry," she reassured him as she continued through the swinging doors, "I'm not selling."

"You better not!" he called after her.

"You better not what?" asked Kelsey as Mandy cleared the door and crossed over to the sink to wash her hands.

"Sell. Brock Anderson told Auntie Anna today there's a buyer for the land," she explained.

"That's not new, is it?"

"Not to me, but it was to her," Mandy said with a frown. "I wish he hadn't said anything to her. It made her think I only stay in Harmony to take care of her, not because I want to."

"Which is silly. You stay here to take care of all of us!" Kelsey retorted. "Seriously, you've got a great business and a wonderful BFF who works for you in said business. What more could you want?"

"No idea." Mandy laughed. "Seems you've covered most of it."

"And we know who stirred that pot, right? Your hottie architect friend."

"He's not my hottie architect friend. And Brock didn't come out and tell her so, but yeah, I'm sure it's him."

"What are you going to do about it?" Kelsey uncovered the cake layers they had stored in the fridge overnight to get them ready for the fondant Mandy would apply shortly.

"Do about what?" Suzette walked back from where she had stashed her coat and backpack in Mandy's office, phone in hand. "Here, Mandy, it's for you." She then perched on the stool next to Kelsey. "What'd I miss?" she asked in a whisper as Kelsey shushed her.

"Hello, this is Mandy—" Mandy pulled the receiver away from her ear. "They hung up."

"Again?" Kelsey's eyebrows went up. "I got one of those this morning. When I told the person you weren't here she hung up."

"I had one of those yesterday," Suzette commented. "And I think Zak did too, or it might have been the day before. Weird. What did I miss?"

"You missed where Mandy is going to tell us her plan to convince her hottie architect he can't buy her land." Kelsey smirked at her employer.

"He's not my hot— Never mind. I don't have a plan. I don't need a plan. I'll simply ignore him." Mandy poked at the fondant sitting in its cling wrap on the counter. Finding it soft enough, she grabbed the canister of confectioner's sugar from in front of Kelsey and lightly covered the surface of the table so she could roll out the icing.

"Of course you need a plan! Ignoring him isn't going to make him go away. You have to convince him he's wrong and you're right."

"Oh, yeah, like he's going to back down and admit he's wrong." Mandy rolled her eyes as she smoothed out the fondant and checked for bubbles. "I don't think so."

"No, that's what the plan is for. He won the fancy catered dinner in the silent auction. That's your opportunity to strut your stuff. You're going to completely *wow* him with your business savvy and your fabulous cooking and your sexy self. And—"

"Wait, wait, wait! This is a professional gig for me. There will be no 'strutting of stuff.' And it's kind of hard to be sexy in a chef's jacket." Happy with the thickness of the fondant, Mandy unwrapped her baking straightedge to measure and cut the square she would need for the first cake layer.

"No, see, that's the beauty of it. He'll never suspect a thing! You're going to seduce him with food. And then—"

"Then, nothing," Mandy declared. "Have you forgotten this is a fancy dinner for two? He's going to have a guest." She shook her head and started on the second ball of fondant.

Kelsey huffed impatiently. "Maybe, maybe not. You can still flirt with him. Not so much that you piss off his guest, but enough to make the evening interesting. It's the food you want to be the star, right? And food always tastes better in excellent surroundings. A little music, a little light banter… He'll never know what hit him."

"I thought she wants him to know what hit him. If he doesn't know what hit him, then he could be having dinner anywhere, cooked by anyone. Don't we want him to know Mandy Brighton of Whimsy created this exclusively for him?" asked Suzette.

Kelsey turned to the girl. "That's the part she'll have to play by ear. As soon as Mandy gets there she can scope out the situation and figure out how to stage this." She spun on her stool. "Unless you want me to come with? At least for setup and prep? I could—"

"*No!* No, no, no. Bad idea. Really, really bad idea." Mandy almost moaned at the thought of Kelsey coming to the dinner with her and trying to give stage directions. "I can handle dinner."

"Yes, you can! And that's the point. It's not merely about delivering his silent auction win. It's about showing him how talented you are—*in the kitchen!*" She laughed at Mandy's expression of horror. "You're trying to show him how successful your business is, right? And how valuable this location, this family-owned piece of property, is to that business, right? And how you don't need to move to Calgary to grow Whimsy into more than the really excellent cupcake bakery it already is, right? So as you prep and serve dinner, you give him a running commentary about how you want to expand into the yarn shop space when Connie Miller retires this summer, and start serving breakfast and lunch, and do some catering, and that's why you're doing this dinner, to show off your catering. He'll get the idea pretty quick you know what you're doing."

Suzette stared at her. "Amazing. I don't think you took a single breath in that whole speech."

"What's more amazing is that it'll work. You'll see, Mandy," Kelsey declared. "By the time dessert rolls around, you'll have him eating out of the palm of your hand. Pun intended."

Mandy frowned at her friend's smirk. "And if he isn't?"

"Then you go with plan B."

"Which is?"

"Sleep with him."

Chapter Nine

Dinner was excellent. Mandy always enjoyed eating at the Thurston Hotel. Even for a large banquet, Chef Guy put out one heck of a meal—not an easy feat.

The two Diamond rooms had been opened up into one big ballroom, and beautifully decorated for the occasion. Mandy admired her surroundings as she passed by the empty dance floor on her way back to her seat from the ladies' room. *Wendy's outdone herself. I'm glad Harmony has a place like this for fancy events. But I'm glad they're going to renovate!*

The crystal chandeliers were toned down enough so you couldn't see the faded carpet and drapes, or the worn spots on the seat covers. But the candles shone bright, and the fresh flowers on the tables scented the air.

The hall glittered almost as much as the people in it. She appreciated being a pretty good fit right off the rack. Katherine Keeler's Sleek Chic dress shop offered a terrific selection for a small town on the edge of the Rocky Mountains, and Mandy hadn't had to go into Calgary to find a dress she liked.

"Are you ready for the big announcement?" asked Wendy as Mandy took her seat.

Mandy rolled her eyes. "I don't know why this has to be a big deal. I know he won the bid, he knows he won the bid, the whole town knows he won the bid! Can't they mention us both from the podium and be done with it?"

"Absolutely not," came a voice from behind her. "Your dinner was far and away the most successful silent auction entry. You made my fundraiser a success, and we want to recognize you for it. Besides"—Katherine smirked—"it's good advertising for Sleek Chic to get you up in front of everybody wearing a dress from my shop!"

"Seriously? This is advertising for you? Why don't you pin a sign on her back, 'Dress from Sleek Chic,' and be done with it?" Wendy said.

"No, no, no, we must be subtle here. But between your dress, Mandy, and yours, Wendy, and mine, and Riley and her mother telling everyone where her wedding dress will come from, I'm getting pretty good exposure tonight." Katherine breathed on her fingernails and buffed them against her own cocktail dress.

Her gesture made Mandy laugh. She knew perfectly well that exposure for Sleek Chic came a distant second on Katherine's agenda tonight. Although she had no children of her own, Katherine contributed to anything benefiting Harmony's youngsters. Raising funds to renovate an outdated playground was near and dear to her heart. "All right. Can we get this over with?" she asked.

"Why? You in a hurry? Got a hot date after?" teased Wendy.

"No, but an early morning. Bakers are early risers. I usually get down to the kitchen around 4 a.m. Late nights don't mix well with early mornings."

"We're waiting for the mayor to— Oh, there he goes. I'm up next," Katherine said, excusing herself and making her way between the tables toward the podium.

Mandy listened with half an ear as the mayor talked about the playground and the grants paying for most of it, and then introduced Katherine and her fundraiser. She idly ran her eyes over the crowd, finding first her Auntie Anna sitting with some of her cronies from Pineview, then Mrs. A and Emily Jamieson.

A large male body interrupted her view across the dance floor. Kevin MacNeal edged around the chairs at her table and dropped into one next to her. "Ready for your moment in the spotlight?"

She shot him a dirty look. "Why does everyone keep asking me that?"

"I think everyone I talked to tonight has asked me the same thing. I figured they wanted to rattle the new kid in class," he explained. "Glad to hear it's not only me."

Mandy shook her head as she finished her wine. "It's not only you. What can I do for you tonight, Mr. MacNeal?"

"It's Kevin. If we're going to be spending an evening together, don't you think we can dispense with the formalities? I think—"

Whatever he thought, it would have to wait for later, as Katherine summoned them both to the podium. Kevin surprised Mandy when he stood quickly and held her chair as she rose. He then took her elbow as they walked up the side of the room to the podium, casually steering her up the side of the hall.

Except, she couldn't classify what she felt at his touch as anything near casual. Her arm heated where his hand rested, even as goose bumps raced from the spot to cover her upper body. Her hearing closed down to two things: her pulse in her eardrums, and his breathing. She drew in a quick breath and shivered.

"Cold?" His murmur stirred the tendrils of hair against her neck.

Mandy shivered again and shook her head. Good thing they were close to the front of the room, as she couldn't have formulated an intelligible response if the fate of the world rested on it. Her tongue stuck to the roof of her very dry mouth.

She pulled away and poured a glass of water from the pitcher on the bar by the podium. Kevin waited for her to drink down most of it. "You okay?"

"She'll be fine," Wendy said, her stage whisper carrying almost as far as her regular voice. "Mandy's not a fan of public speaking." The older woman herded both of them to where Katherine Keeler waited with Mayor Hamilton.

The mayor grabbed Kevin's hand and shook it as Katherine introduced the architect as the winning bidder on the "elegant dinner for two donated by Whimsy." "The town of Harmony wants to extend its sincere thanks to you for your generous donation to our playground fund, your bid in our silent auction. Ladies and gentlemen, Kevin MacNeal!"

Kevin stepped to the microphone. "Thank you, everyone. As the new guy in town, I appreciate the opportunity to participate in this worthy venture. But the real thanks should go to Mandy Brighton, who graciously supplied the dinner package I bid on." He reached for her hand and tugged a reluctant Mandy to his side as the crowd applauded again.

Who knew a fear of public speaking could be a good thing? Mandy attributed her shaking hands to the crowd in front of her, and not to the man at her side—the man whose subtle scent reminded her of spruce trees and cold mountain mornings.

She cleared her throat a few times. "Um, thanks, everyone. At Whimsy we believe in supporting our community whenever we can, so of course I contributed something to the silent auction."

She handed the mike to Katherine and backed up—straight into a hard male chest. His quiet chuckle vibrated through her and she almost missed the question from the mayor. "Oh! Sorry, I didn't catch your question, Ed."

"That's all right, I can take this one," said Kevin smoothly. He took the mike back as if he gave speeches in small towns all the time. "No, we haven't talked about a date yet, or the menu. I know Whimsy is famous for their cupcakes, but I'm a meat and potatoes kind of guy, so I hope there'll be more than dessert!"

Katherine laughed and took the mike back. "You won't have any worries there. Mandy is planning to expand Whimsy and open a breakfast and lunch café. Isn't that right, Mandy?"

Mandy nodded but didn't have a chance to speak as Katherine continued: "And you want to offer catering as well. People of Harmony, consider this her first foray into full meal service, with many more to come. I'm sure she'll keep us all posted." The audience applauded as Katherine acknowledged them one more time, shaking both their hands in obvious dismissal.

As he escorted Mandy back to her table, Kevin asked, "You're planning to expand into another location? Off the main strip, I assume?"

"No, right next door. I plan to take over Connie Miller's space when she retires and renovate it, and expand up into the two apartments. I'll add a commercial kitchen for the café and catering business, and they can share some resources with Whimsy. I don't know exactly when, though. Connie hasn't decided whether to try and sell her business or close it."

"If she sells it, how can you expand next door? Won't the new owner want to rent the same space?"

"Not an option. The lease isn't part of the business. Connie's talking with the owner of the quilt shop on the other side about somehow combining the two businesses into one space, which empties the middle bay."

They had reached her seat, but Kevin didn't seem to be in any rush to rejoin his table on the other side of the room. Mandy stood awkwardly, waiting for him to finish asking her about her business, waiting for the butterflies in her stomach to calm down. Usually only speaking in front of a crowd made her nervous, not one-on-one conversations.

Of course, she didn't spend a lot of time talking to men who made her pulse flutter like a frightened bird. Or her hands itch with the desire to reach out and touch... *Wait. What?* Mandy stopped her hand before it moved more than an inch from where it hung by her side.

She cleared her throat. She'd been doing that a lot tonight, but her voice kept squeaking. "Look, I, um..."

"Dance with me?"

"What?"

"Dance with me. You know, go out on the dance floor, stand close together, sway to the music, have a conversation... Dance with me."

She hadn't even heard the music start. *He must think I'm an idiot.* "I hadn't planned to stay long once Katherine made her announcements."

"Come on. One dance. We should settle on a date for dinner, talk about the menu. Get to know one another a little, don't you think?"

"I—"

He took her hand and started for the dance floor. "Come on. One dance. What could it hurt?"

It didn't. Hurt, that was. In fact, Mandy couldn't remember when she'd enjoyed herself so much. One dance turned into two, then three. They talked about a date for the dinner (next weekend), and the menu (Irish food, for St. Patrick's Day and for Kevin's Irish heritage). They talked about the people in town she knew and he was getting to know (Brock Anderson and Riley Hamilton; Riley's parents, Mayor Ed Hamilton and his wife, Lilith; Mrs. A and her circle of friends).

Brock cut in on their fourth dance, sending Riley off with Kevin. "Good to see you sticking around and enjoying yourself, Mandy. Riley says you work too hard."

"Not really. But I have to get up early, which makes late nights not such a good idea. In fact, I should think about leaving soon." She glanced at her watch.

"Oh, no, you don't. You're not leaving right after I dance with you. Kevin will think I ticked you off and you left. And Riley would kill me. You don't want that to happen, do you?"

He teased, she knew, but still she felt guilty for something she hadn't even done yet. "No, of course not."

"Good." He danced her around another couple. "Has he talked to you about your building yet?"

"Not in so many words." She let him steer them to a less crowded corner of the dance floor. "He's talked around it, asked about the business some, especially when he heard I want to expand. He hasn't mentioned whether he knows who owns the building and the land."

"I'm going to assume if he did ask if the family is interested in selling, the answer is no."

"That's right. My business is doing really well there. Even if I didn't want to expand, why would I sell? Whimsy and I are there effectively rent-free. The other rentals more than cover the insurance and taxes, and give Auntie Anna a good retirement income. Sure, if we sold she'd have a whack of cash to invest, but I don't think she wants to have to think about managing her finances. This is easy for her, and it works."

"That's what I thought," Brock confirmed.

"He hasn't gone as far as talking about making an actual offer for the land, has he?"

"No, but I wouldn't be surprised if he does once the town hall renovations and the new community center are well underway. He's got a pool of potential investors, remember? They're going to want to see something tangible happening on Main Street before they commit."

"So you think I've got some time to convince him it's a bad idea?"

Brock shrugged. "I don't know if you'll ever convince him it's a bad idea. You can probably convince him it isn't going to happen."

They circled back around the floor and ended the dance next to their respective partners. Mandy found herself enveloped in a hug from Riley. "I know you won't stay much later, Mandy, so I'll say good night now!" And she and Brock stepped back out onto the dance floor.

"I should really head out. I have to be up early," Mandy explained as she started to back away.

"I can't talk you into one more dance?"

She shouldn't, she really shouldn't. It was already after 10 p.m., and she had to be up and in the bakery in less than six hours.

"All right, one more. But only one! Or I'll fall asleep in a bowl of cake batter in the morning."

Kevin laughed as he spun her out onto the floor. "Well, we can't have that, can we? The good citizens of Harmony would run me out of town on a rail if they couldn't get their cupcakes in the morning."

"See? That's why I won't move out of Harmony. I'd never get such customer loyalty in a big city like Calgary."

"Maybe not. But you'd have a much bigger population base to draw from, so it wouldn't be so much of an issue."

"Not for you, maybe. Look, in your business, you come in, do a project, and leave, right? I live here. My customers are my friends. I've made a wedding cake for a couple and a year or two later, I make the cake for their baby shower or christening. When I expand by opening the café, I'll be able to offer people a place to have those parties, one a little more affordable than a banquet room here in the Thurston Hotel. Not every bride is as well-off as Riley Hamilton, with parents who can afford the best place in town. Sometimes a smaller place is perfect."

"You've thought about this."

"Of course I have! I'm very careful with my business. I don't do anything at Whimsy without thinking it through first. I lived too many years with too much uncertainty. I'll make changes, but I don't take risks."

"What uncertainty? You walked in and took over a family business. Not much uncertainty or risk there," he commented.

Mandy looked up at him in amazement. "Is that what you think? My great-aunt and great-uncle handed me the business? I didn't have to work to make Whimsy what it is?" She turned away and walked back to her table. "You don't know me at all," she said, picking up her evening bag and heading for the door.

"Hey, wait! I didn't say you didn't work for it. But you have to admit, the fact your family owned the bakery made it easier for you to start your own business. You didn't start from scratch."

She whirled and faced him. "Maybe you ought to check your facts. I did start Whimsy from scratch, when Auntie Anna and Uncle Joe retired. I took out a loan to buy their equipment and add more. I pay rent along with the other tenants. I don't pull income from the family corporation, only she does." She shook her head in disgust and started walking again. "Let me know what time you want me to show up Saturday. I'll need about an hour to finish prepping before I start to serve."

"Look, I'm sorry, okay? It's just..." Kevin ran his hand through his hair, looking uncertain. "I guess I don't understand small-town dynamics. And you make your business success look so effortless it's easy for an outsider to underestimate how much work you've put into it."

Mandy slowed down as she reached the door to make one final comment. "Maybe if you want to do more small-town municipal projects, you might make an effort to get to know us a little better. In the meantime, don't make judgments about things you don't understand."

Chapter Ten

Mandy split her stack of various-sized cupcake boxes, dropping a few right next to Zak and sorting the rest into their slots on the shelf under the register. "This should hold you through the afternoon, Zak. We got a shipment Friday so there's more in the back if you need them."

"Thanks, Mandy," he said, deftly assembling a flattened cardboard shape into a box before placing two Lucky Shamrock cupcakes inside and handing it to the customer. "There you are, two to go. Are these for our visiting architect? I thought you picked up his order this morning, Jake?"

"Nah, these are for my daughters." The big construction worker laughed as he paid. "They figured out I come here for coffee and cupcakes when they found the stash of empty wrappers in my truck. They've been on my case ever since to bring some for them. Figured I'd pop back in and grab a couple of fresh ones on my way home. I thought maybe I could get them to wash the truck and pay them in cupcakes."

"Wait, whose order did you say you picked up this morning, Jake?" Mandy had missed that snippet of their conversation and was genuinely curious, as most of the guys who stopped in every morning never made it out the door with their cupcakes. They consumed them on the spot.

"MacNeal's. Last week he started a standing order for two cupcakes every morning," Jake replied. "He still runs home to the Thurston for his fancy coffee, but he's hooked on your cupcakes."

Zak waggled his eyebrows at Mandy. "What did you do to make him change his mind, hmmm?"

"Me? Nothing. In fact, I would have thought... Never mind." She stepped out from around Zak and headed for the kitchen.

"Stop right there," Zak called. "You don't get to say something like that and disappear. Spill."

Mandy paused with one foot through the swinging door and glanced longingly into the other room. She ignored the jangle of the sleigh bells as the outer door opened behind her, saying, "We had... a bit of a disagreement at the fundraising dance on Saturday. Really, guys, it was nothing," she protested at the murmured responses. "I'm surprised he's ordering cupcakes, that's all. You do notice he's still not coming in for them, right?"

"Um, Mandy..."

"No, really, guys. What's wrong with Whimsy? Too girly? Sheesh, Jake, you come in every day. Doesn't seem to hurt your manly self-image any to eat a cupcake from a pink-and-white wrapper in public." She shook her head, ignoring Zak's panicked look over her shoulder.

Until the sound of a throat clearing behind her made her squeeze her eyes shut. "Oh, crap. He's behind me, isn't he?" she murmured to Zak.

At his cautious nod, she turned around to face the music. "Mr. MacNeal. What brings you here today?"

Kevin looked almost as embarrassed as she felt. "Can I talk to you? Without everyone listening?" He rubbed the back of his neck and didn't quite meet her gaze.

"Sure." She owed him that much for her outburst. Glaring at Zak, she swept past the gaggle of construction workers and led the way to the little café table farthest from the register and the crowd. "Can I get you a coffee or anything?"

"No, thanks anyway. I won't take much of your time."

For someone who looked so anxious to talk to her, he seemed reluctant to say anything. She'd have to get this ball rolling. She only hoped it didn't roll right over her. "Look, Mr. MacNeal, I'm sorry. I shouldn't have—"

"Kevin. Please, call me Kevin. And you don't need to apologize. That's what I came in here for, to apologize to you. Things didn't exactly end on a high note on Saturday."

"No, they didn't. And I'm sorry too. But I meant what I said, about getting to understand small towns better before you start making recommendations to change what's working."

"I know you did." He shifted in the small chair. "And that's the other thing I wanted to talk to you about. I'm in Harmony mostly as the architect for the town hall and community center, but they also asked me to consult on commercial development in the town in general. All I can do is tell them what I know, based on what I've seen on other projects in other small towns."

"And we're all the same, these small towns of your experience?"

"For the most part, yes. What a community can do has a lot to do with population size and tax base. So if Harmony is different," he said, speaking over her indrawn breath, "if Harmony is different, convince me."

"What?"

"Convince me." Kevin leaned forward, resting his arms on the table. "Let's have a conversation not on a dance floor or in your place of work. Or mine, for that matter. Why don't you have dinner with me, and we can talk about it?"

Mandy's mind raced even as her face blushed, the curse of the fair complexion she inherited from her German ancestors. "Dinner? With you? *Like a date?*" She didn't realize she'd spoken the last bit aloud until he responded.

"Think of it more like a business meeting with a meal. A nice quiet dinner, anyway. Away from this," he said, waving his hand at the people still milling around the register and making no secret of their attempts to hear what Mandy and Kevin were saying.

"Oh. Well. I hadn't thought—"

"You do eat dinner, don't you?" His quick grin charmed her even more for its sudden, unexpected appearance. "A girl can't survive on cupcakes alone, even ones as good as yours."

She could only stare for a few seconds. Then, before she thought herself out of it, she replied, "Sure. I'm not free tonight, but… tomorrow, maybe?"

"Sounds good. Tomorrow is better for me than Thursday or Friday; I have to head back to Calgary for a day or so. Do you like Italian? The pasta place on Elk Street is pretty good; I've been eating there at least once a week since I've been in town. Or if not there—"

"No, no, that's fine. Pasta Italia's great. I know the owners."

Kevin rose. "Good. Great. Tomorrow at seven thirty," he said as they walked toward the door. "I'll pick you up."

"Oh, no, that's okay. I figured I'd walk over." Mandy pressed her hand against her belly in a vain attempt to calm the jittery feeling creeping through her. "It's only a block once I'm through the parking lot."

"Walking sounds good. How about I make a reservation for seven thirty and swing by here at quarter after or so?"

"You don't have to. I can meet—"

"My mother would have my head if I let you walk by yourself at night. I'll see you tomorrow about seven fifteen." He nodded at Zak and headed out.

The bells over the door jangled behind him. Zak had managed to disperse the crowd of construction workers at some point, so only he heard Kevin's parting remark.

"Tomorrow at seven fifteen? What's tomorrow at seven fifteen?" At times like this, when Zak bounced up and down like an eager puppy, it struck Mandy how the few years between them made so much difference. Especially a few years of running a bakery and owning rental properties and watching out for her great-aunt. A few years of responsibility were enough to reinforce her natural caution.

She pushed past him and through the doors into the kitchen. "Dinner, apparently."

"Wait. What? Dinner?" He pushed through right behind her and followed her over to where she plunked herself down on a stool and dropped her head into her hands.

"Dinner? What dinner? Who's having dinner?" piped up Kelsey.

"Our boss. With the hottie architect." Zak faked wiping a tear from his eye. "I'm so proud."

"What? You're kidding!"

"When?"

"Why?"

"Who asked who?"

Kelsey and Suzette fired staccato questions at them from across the big worktable.

Zak raised his hands to stop the barrage. "Not kidding. Tomorrow night. And… I don't know why. I mean, other than because he's the hottie architect. And because he asked his cupcake girl out on a date."

"I really wish you'd stop calling me that." Mandy's muffled voice came from the cradle of her arms. "I'm not his cupcake girl. And it isn't a date, it's a business dinner."

"Uh huh. And if you believe that, I've got some land to sell you… Oh, wait. Maybe it is a business dinner. Is this about the land, you think?" Zak pulled out the stool next to

Mandy. "Is that why you said yes, to pump him for information?"

"Yes. No. I don't know." She lifted her head and looked at him sideways. "He caught me by surprise, is all."

"So, this is like... a whim? You said yes to dinner on a whim?" Suzette came around the table and took the stool on Mandy's other side. "But you never do anything on a whim. You are the queen of planning, deliberation, and organization. You are my hero. You're my mother's hero, because since I started working here I've been keeping my room neater."

"And she'll be even more your hero when she sticks to the plan and uses this opportunity to make him fall at her feet," Kelsey declared. She came around behind Mandy and started rubbing her shoulders. "Jeez, these are like rocks. Relax! It's dinner. It's another chance to work the plan."

"This is the plan where our boss the hero seduces the big bad hottie architect and convinces him buying her land is a terrible idea?" asked Zak. "I remember that plan. It's a good plan. You listen to her, boss," he declared, jumping off his stool at the jingle of the bells on the shop door. "Kelsey is wise in the way of using sex to get what she wants."

"Hey!" Kelsey grabbed a towel from the counter and flicked it at him on his way by.

The towel missed as he sidestepped and pushed through the door. "Okay, charm, not sex. It's a compliment, Kels. We admire that in you. You're the best one to give her lessons."

"I'm not going to seduce him," Mandy warned.

"Not tomorrow, no. Tomorrow is for softening him up. Then later you seduce him."

"It's dinner. A business dinner. He says he wants to understand what makes Harmony tick and why I think his redevelopment is a bad idea. That's all."

"But it's a lead-in for the dinner you're going to make for him for Saturday, right? You can start the discussion tomorrow, give him a few days to think about it, and then hammer it home when you cook him dinner," Suzette said slowly, thinking it through. "I like it."

"And that's a fancy dinner for two. Not for one. You think he's going to be at all interested in talking about business with me when he has a date there for a cozy evening in? I don't think so."

"What makes you think he'll have a date for your dinner?" countered Kelsey.

"Because he bid on a dinner for two? And because he's going to Calgary Thursday or Friday, presumably to bring back his date for Saturday?"

"Maybe. We'll see. I bet he doesn't, though. Bring anybody back, that is. He's not dating anyone." Kelsey sat, then swiveled back and forth on her stool as she dropped her little gem.

"How do you even know these things?"

"He said something to Jason Knight, the bartender at the Thurston Lounge, and Jason told Brock Anderson, and Brock told Riley, and Riley told—"

"Never mind. I should have known the Harmony grapevine would be all over him."

"What do you expect? Small town, new guy in said small town expresses interest in one of Harmony's leading businesswomen, and there you go!"

"While I appreciate being named one of Harmony's leading businesswomen, even if you're the only one who voted, said new guy has not expressed any interest in me. Only in my land."

"And you still believe that? Even after he outbid everyone so he could get you to cook for him? And then he got too impatient waiting for the dinner he already bought, so he asked you out days ahead of time?" Kelsey shook her head. "For a smart, savvy businesswoman, you can be dense sometimes. Where is he taking you?"

"Pasta Italia, Zak said," answered Suzette.

"See? For a business dinner he'd take you to the Thurston Lounge or the Foothills Dining Room. Instead he chooses one of the most romantic places in town."

"Oh, man." Mandy dropped her head back down into her arms. "Why did I say yes, again?"

"For once, you did something you wanted to do without worrying about the repercussions or implications. For once," Kelsey said, nudging her, "you did something on a whim."

Chapter Eleven

Kelsey looked up as Mandy walked back into the kitchen. "That's an odd look on your face. Everything okay with your great-aunt? Who was on the phone?" She placed a wrapper into the last cup in the mold and dropped the rest back into their plastic tub.

"What? Oh, no, nothing's wrong with Auntie Anna. That was Kevin MacNeal, calling about tonight." Mandy wandered over to the table and peered into the bowl of batter. "Want me to pour these or start the next batch?"

Her friend pushed the tins over. "You pour, I'll mix. What did your hottie architect want?"

"To cancel tonight." Mandy grabbed the ice cream scoop they used to portion out each cupcake and started scooping and filling the paper cups.

"What? Why? Jeez, he made such a big thing about coming in and apologizing and asking you out, you'd think he'd want to keep the date." Kelsey shook her head as she measured the flour. "Why did he cancel?"

"He had to go back to Calgary a day early for some meeting. Called me from his car; he's already halfway there."

"I still think it's rude." Dry ingredients ready to go, Kelsey pulled up the mixer on its stand and dumped butter into the bowl. "Did he at least cancel the reservations, so Pasta Italia can free up the table? Not that it matters so much on a weeknight, but it's only polite."

"Even better. He called them to change it over to my name, and told me to go anyway and he'd cover the bill." Mandy rapped the filled tins on the counter to bounce out any bubbles, then slid them into a wall oven and set the timer. "Not sure I'm going to go, but it was a nice gesture."

"That's more like it! Take your Auntie Anna. I bet she'd enjoy dinner there." Kelsey flipped on the mixer to cream the butter with sugar, then added eggs one at a time.

"Actually," Mandy said, raising her voice to be heard over the noisy machine, "is Brian working tonight? Why don't the two of you go? I'll watch the kidlets."

Her employee's face lit up, then fell. "Are you sure? Two is more than twice as hard as one. They're a little rambunctious when they get home from day care. Evenings can be a challenge."

Mandy waved off the half-hearted protest. "Sure. Call Brian to set it up." She looked at the clock over the door to the adjoining shop. "It's almost five. And Suzette's here till closing. Once that batter is mixed, why don't you go get them and go home a little early? Go grab a shower, get ready, and I'll come by around seven or so."

"Once again, are you sure?" Kelsey shook her head. "This isn't like you."

"What, I don't do favors for my friends?"

"No, not that. Acting so impulsively isn't like you. You've always been the calm, steady one. I'm more of the spur-of-the-moment girl."

"And aren't you the one who always tells me I should think less and act more? Do things on a whim? That's what you said when I accepted the dinner invitation from Kevin in the first place," Mandy reminded her.

"It's true, I did say that. I didn't expect you to take it to heart so fast! I figured you'd have to ease into it."

"You mean the way you eased into yoga with me? When was the last time you came to class with me?"

"That's different. You are naturally more flexible than I am. And you need the classes more than I do."

"Hey, watch it! Are you saying I need to work out more?" Mandy grabbed a handful of flour from the bin at her side and threw it at Kelsey.

"Noooo, didn't mean that. But chasing after two kids is a full-body workout. And carrying one around who doesn't walk yet does wonders for strengthening your core." She snickered as she took off her apron and brushed off the flour. "You'll see tonight. You won't need to go to class tomorrow. You might even be too sore to go for a couple of days!"

Mandy smiled as she shooed her friend out the door. Sending Kelsey and Brian to the restaurant was less of a whim than the other woman imagined. If she went herself, or with her great-aunt, she'd be explaining all night to half the town why she was there for a business dinner with Kevin, without Kevin. This way, Kelsey and Brian got a nice evening out, and Mandy didn't have to run the gauntlet of Harmony's oh-so-friendly (read *nosy*) citizens.

"Two birds, one stone," she murmured as she finished up Kelsey's last batch of cupcakes and got them in the oven.

She was still congratulating herself when the swinging doors cracked open. "Where's Kelsey?" Zak peered around the edge. "I thought she was on till seven tonight."

"Just sent her home to get ready for date night with Brian," Mandy explained, setting up to make the frosting she'd need when the cupcakes cooled.

"They have a date night too? Some coincidence. Who's watching the kidlets?"

"No coincidence. I'm going over there to watch them around seven. Can you and Suzette close up?"

"Of course, but why are you not going out with your hottie architect? I thought the two of you were going to Pasta Italia tonight, to talk 'business.'" Zak smirked as he made the air quotes. "Monkey business, maybe!"

"Smart ass. It was going to be a business dinner, but he got called back to Calgary a day early. Kels and Brian are taking the reservation. Which leaves me to babysit."

"Both at once? You're braver than I am." He shuddered. "I like kids better when they get old enough to be in school most of the day."

"Coward. Hers are cute. Question for you: Would you say I'm too cautious?"

Zak came all the way into the kitchen. "Is this a trick question?"

"No, I'm serious here. Kelsey said something about me tending to overthink. Do I come across as never being spontaneous, that I'm too rigid?"

"Mmm, not never, but not real often either. I wouldn't call you rigid. Cautious, maybe. Unlike Kelsey who rarely looks before she leaps, you do tend to think things through first. But not to worry," he said with a grin, "you have us to keep you from getting too serious. And having a fling with the hottie architect definitely qualifies as doing something on a whim!"

Chapter Twelve

Kevin swept his glance over his hotel suite one more time. Fresh flowers: check. Table set for dinner, complete with lit candles: check. TV tuned to a classic rock station, set low: check. He'd staged the scene with everything but the dinner itself. That would arrive with Mandy.

A tentative knock drew his attention. He crossed the room and pulled open the door.

"Right on time," he greeted his nervous-looking visitor. "Wow, don't you look… official."

She tugged at the hem of her chef's jacket. "I, um, yes. This is a working dinner for me, the first of many, I hope. May I come in?"

"Of course." He stepped back and held the door wide as she rolled in a large covered trolley. "That's a lot of food for two people."

"It's not all food," Mandy replied. She steered the trolley past his toes and into the kitchen area of the suite. "The only suite I've been in up here is Mrs. A's, so I didn't know what equipment would be in this one. Plus there's wine." She unlatched the side panels, removing them and leaning them against the wall by the door, and started emptying the cart onto the counter.

"Can I help?" Kevin peered over her shoulder, standing close, crowding her a little. There were a lot of shapes in her trolley he didn't recognize, and they were all, it seemed, going to come out and play.

"Here, you can put these two in the freezer. And then these in the fridge." She made quick work of sorting and stacking everything else, including a collection of wine in smaller demi-bottles. "I hope your guest likes the menu we talked about."

"No guest. Just us."

"No guest?" She spun on her heel, stopping her momentum against the counter. "This is a dinner for two, remember? I figured that's why you went to Calgary, to collect your guest for the evening."

He took the last bottles of wine from her hands and lined them up on the counter with the others. "If that's your way of asking if I'm seeing someone, the answer is no, I'm not. I thought tonight would be another opportunity to talk. Privately this time, without half the town butting in."

"Oh. Well." Mandy stood with a saucepan in her hand and looked at everything on the counter. She huffed out a breath and glanced at him. "I'm not exactly sure how to do dinner, then. I had it planned and timed so you and your guest would be eating one course while I prepared the next one."

"Why don't I help you cook?" He grinned. "Maybe I'll learn to make something more than mac 'n' cheese."

"Oh, please don't tell me you make it from a box! Seriously?" Mandy shook her head. She emptied a container of bright-green liquid into the saucepan and turned on the burner. "Why don't you open the sparkling wine, and I'll get the watercress soup ready."

"Watercress soup? Not salad?" Kevin worked the wire cage off the bottle and eased out the cork with a gentle pop. He poured and handed a glass to Mandy, who nodded her thanks before sipping.

"When I was young and living with my mom, we didn't eat a lot of vegetables. Whenever I stayed here, my great-aunt worked hard to get greens into me. She hid a lot of stuff in soups and sauces." She fished a clean spoon from a drawer and tasted the contents of the pot before rinsing off the spoon. "Could you hand me the salt?"

He kept hold of the salt grinder, letting her tug him closer until less than an inch separated them. "Here, I'll trade you the salt for a taste."

Mandy blushed as she dipped the clean spoon back into the soup. She blushed even more when he took her hand and guided the spoon to his mouth for a taste. "Mmm. Delicious."

Kevin felt the temperature in the room rise several degrees, and not from the heat of the stove. Who knew a chef's jacket and clunky shoes could look sexy?

He rubbed his thumb against her fingers where they held the spoon. "Mandy?"

"Yeah?"

"The pot is going to boil over."

"Oh!" She abandoned the spoon, whirling to lift the saucepan off the burner and stir the soup with a whisk. "I, um, are there soup bowls on the table?" Her words came out in a shivery rush.

"Want me to get them?" Kevin eased away from her side and walked to the table. He chuckled at the whoosh of released breath behind him as he collected the bowls and brought them to her.

"You mentioned living with your mom and staying here, as if they were different. You're so much a part of this town, I had thought you grew up here." He picked up his sparkling wine again for a sip.

She waggled her hand back and forth, yes-no, as she turned the oven on to preheat. "Sort of. My mother had me before she turned seventeen. Auntie Anna and Uncle Joe took her in when her parents threw her out. I was born here, and we lived with them for the first few years. But Mom never could stay in one place very long. She'd take off for months on end. As I got older she started taking me with her. I remember traveling around a lot, missing weeks of school, or going to school in one place for a couple of months, then switching to a new one. Sometimes we'd end up back here and stay for a while, or she'd dump me off for a stretch."

Kevin placed his glass down gently. He didn't want to snap the delicate stem. But who did that to their kid? No wonder Mandy felt so tied to the town. She had spent the best parts of her growing-up years here, and Harmony was the only real home she'd known.

He took a steadying breath. Her situation, her past, couldn't be allowed to influence his decision to go after her land. But maybe finding out more would give him the key to changing her mind. "You learned to cook from your great-aunt and her husband?"

"Yep. Auntie Anna cooked, and Uncle Joe baked. Which is funny, because the bakery came down through her side of the family. I spent a lot of time in kitchens with them. Learned to make bread before I was tall enough to see into the big mixers." She tasted the soup one more time. "This is almost ready to go." She ladled portions into bowls, ground black pepper over the tops, and swirled on dollops of crème fraîche before taking them to the table and pulling out her chair.

"Smells amazing." He topped up their glasses with the last of the small bottle of wine. "Tell me more about growing up in a bakery."

Their conversation over soup ranged from trading childhood memories, to different kinds of bread from different parts of the world, to cooking shows on TV. Kevin loaded the dishwasher with their soup bowls as Mandy started heating up a large cast-iron frying pan. "Wow, I haven't seen one of those since my parents sold their place and moved to Arizona," Kevin commented

"Really? I love cast-iron pans. I've got them in all different sizes." She dropped a lump of butter in the pan and started to melt it. "Do me a favor? Slice the bread, four pieces about this thick," she requested, holding her fingers about a half inch apart, "and toast them."

She finished cooking the mushrooms and other ingredients about the same time he finished toasting the bread. After rubbing the slices with garlic, she mounded them high on two plates with the contents of the frying pan. "Grab a bottle of the white from the fridge, would you?" she asked, delivering the next course of wild mushrooms on toast to the table.

They talked about travel abroad (she had visited more places than he had, which surprised him), they talked about traveling in Canada (he beat her out there), and as they started to delve into Canadian politics, Mandy put the main course together and into the oven. "The vegetables have to go the longest, then the lamb, and then the potatoes. We can finish up this very nice white with some sorbet while the main course cooks. And you can open the red to let it breathe for a bit."

Kevin examined the bottle before working the cork out. "These are some nice wines. Did you go into Calgary for them? I don't remember seeing anything like these at the Thurston."

She brought the small dishes of dark red-orange sorbet to the table. "No, I got them here. You know the liquor store by Bob's Grocery? He'll bring wines in for me if I order by the case. Chef Guy at the Thurston likes to specialize in Canadian wines, but there are a lot of Italian and Spanish wines I like better. Since you said you didn't have any preferences, you get what I like."

Kevin scraped the last of his sorbet from the bowl. "That's really good. I don't recognize the taste."

"Blood orange," Mandy replied, standing to check on the contents of the oven. She gave the vegetables a stir, and turned the racks of lamb over. "Ten more minutes on the lamb, and when it comes out to rest I'll throw the potatoes in."

Two hours later, they were lingering over coffee and the remains of dessert. Kevin polished off his second little pear and cranberry tart, chasing the last of his vanilla bean ice cream with a bit of crust. "This tastes amazing. So this is the kind of thing you want to do, cater dinners like these?" He poured more sweet dessert wine into his glass and motioned toward Mandy's.

"Only a little, thanks. I have to get up early. As for catering dinners like these, yes and no. I like doing the specialty stuff, but what I really want to do is expand Whimsy into a café. I'd rather do breakfast and lunch than dinner."

"How come? I'd have thought the profit is higher on catering than on opening another location. Less overhead." And more portable. Maybe he would be able to convince her to move out of her current space after all. And to Calgary. He stuffed the errant thought down. He didn't care where she moved, as long as it was out of her current building. *Right. You keep thinking that, MacNeal.*

"But you have much later nights. Baking starts early; breakfast is easier than dinner since I'm already there. Speaking of which, I should pack all this up and head out soon. I'll leave you the leftovers."

He stood with her. "Why don't I help you pack it up, and then you can stay for another glass of wine. And didn't I see a box of something we haven't gotten to yet?"

"No, no, I can get it. I'll—"

"Don't be silly. If I help it'll go faster. And then you can help me finish this bottle of… what is this, anyway? Ice wine?" He followed her into the kitchen area and picked up the one remaining box on the counter. "And look, chocolate. What's dessert without chocolate?"

"I hadn't pegged you for a sweet tooth." She ducked out of reach, picking up a stack of her pans and loading them back onto the trolley.

"No? Then why the box of truffles?" He popped one in his mouth, closing his eyes at the explosion of flavor on his tongue. "Oh, man, that's good."

"I included those to leave behind for you and your guest to finish the evening with."

"No guest means more for me. Here, have one so I don't eat them all myself." Kevin plucked a truffle from its little paper cup and held it to her lips.

Mandy's eyes opened with surprise even as her mouth opened to accept the candy. "Oops." He brushed some stray cocoa powder from her bottom lip.

They both froze as his thumb brushed back and forth. "You still have… Let me…" He leaned forward till his lips barely touched hers, once, twice. "Mmm. Tastes sweeter this way."

She pulled in a shaky breath as he leaned back. "That wasn't supposed to happen."

"No?" He trailed his mouth along her jaw to the sensitive spot behind her ear and lingered there. "Why not?" His hands moved from the countertop to her hips, then around her back, pulling her closer.

"It's not… I shouldn't…" Her breath came faster as his lips worked down the side of her neck. She smelled like vanilla and sugar, warm and familiar, both comforting and arousing.

"Shhh." He found her mouth again, kissing her lightly, then not so lightly.

She moaned against him; he deepened the kiss even more. Her hands came up and clutched his shoulders as he pulled her closer.

He tasted; he nibbled. Her mouth rubbed hot and sweet against his. The kiss tasted sumptuous, decadent, and left him wanting more as he eased back, tugging her lower lip into his mouth for a final taste. "I was right. Sweeter this way."

"Kevin, look, I—"

"Don't overthink it, Mandy. It was a kiss." Kevin brushed his mouth against hers one more time. He found it tougher than he expected to release her. The heat from her hands against his chest lingered even after she pulled them away. "Do you want one last glass of wine? Help me finish up this bottle?"

"I'd better not. It'll recork and keep well in the fridge." She stepped back and grabbed one of the side panels, reattaching it to the trolley. "I'd best be going. I want to run this stuff through the dishwasher at the shop tonight."

He helped her maneuver the cart, now much lighter, through the door. "Why don't I help you get all this home? You've got your van here?" At her nod, he continued, "I can always walk back."

"Are you sure? I can manage it myself." But she waited till he had locked his door behind them, he noticed, before pushing the cart toward the elevator.

"Nah, it's fine."

They rode down the service elevator to the basement and continued out through the loading dock. Mandy fetched her van, and they loaded up the trolley and headed for Whimsy.

She used her phone to turn off the alarm as the overhead door lifted, then drove them into the garage at the back of the building. Kevin looked around the space as he helped her roll the trolley out of the van and across the concrete floor, through the storage area, and into the kitchen. "I never realized the building came all the way back here."

"Most of it doesn't. I added the extension when I renovated the rest. Putting the extra refrigerator and freezer and storage out there opened up the kitchen a lot. See?" She gestured to the expansive prep table, multiple ovens, and big gas stove in the corner. "I've still got fridge and freezer space in here, but a lot more room to work too."

Kevin wandered around the shiny kitchen as she loaded up the industrial dishwasher. The space was immaculate, not a bowl or pan out of place, all the surfaces gleaming. "It's a lot bigger than I thought it would be. How many staff do you have now?"

"Two full-time, Zak and Kelsey, and Suzette part-time after school and on weekends. I could use another full-time and another part-time for Whimsy. When I open the café I'll hire even more." With the last of the pans and equipment loaded and the dishwasher set to run, she quickly wiped down the cart and pushed it over into a corner near some closed cabinets. "There, that's the last of it."

"Good." Kevin pulled the partial bottle of dessert wine and the box of truffles from the pockets of his coat. "Why don't we finish these up?"

Mandy eyed him, biting her lip. Then she seemed to come to a decision. "Come with me."

She set the alarm again as she led him out a side door he hadn't noticed, into the hall between the shops, and up a flight of stairs. At the top she used her phone again to turn off the alarm in her apartment. "We'll be more comfortable up here. Let me pour us some wine."

Kevin wandered around the living room as she got some glasses and poured. She had interesting prints on her

117

walls, photographs mostly, of food and restaurants, street scenes from Paris, landscapes of Tuscany or maybe the south of France. And there were books everywhere, covering all sorts of subjects from cooking to travel to the same crime fiction sitting on his bedside table.

It presented an interesting mix, but not as interesting as the woman currently walking toward him carrying glasses of wine and the box of truffles.

He took the glasses and the box from her hands and placed them on the coffee table, taking a seat next to her on the couch. Right next to her, close enough to feel the warmth of her leg against his. And close enough to hear her little gasp as he draped his arm behind her. "Thanks for a great dinner." He played idly with the end of her braid. "I want to see you again."

"Kevin, I'm not sure…"

"Why not?" His breath stirred the wisps of hair at her temple.

She tipped her head back to see his face. "Because you don't live here? You won't be sticking around for long, only until the town hall and community center are built."

"So? Didn't you tell Mrs. A that the way your business is growing, you don't have time for a relationship?"

"Well, yes, but… How did you know that, anyway?"

He kissed the edge of her mouth. "She likes me. She tells me stuff." Kevin tipped up her chin for better access. "Stop talking, Mandy." He could feel her smile against his mouth as he settled it on hers.

The kiss went from playful to steamy in a microsecond. His tongue teased her lips open, then tangled with hers as she moaned and slipped down against the back of the couch.

His arm moved from draping over her shoulders to holding her against him as he leaned in, pressing against her, following her down. Her hands went from clutching his shirt against his chest to sliding around his back and holding on tight.

The kiss went on and on. She tasted like chocolate and the sweet dessert wine and something unmistakably Mandy. Trailing his lips down the side of her throat elicited a throaty moan. Running his hand up her side to cup a breast brought forth a gasp, then a sigh.

He rolled to his side next to her and continued his assault on her mouth. One of his legs worked between hers, pressing her thighs apart and brushing against her most sensitive spot. Mandy moaned again and rocked against him, whispering his name.

Kevin shifted to pull her against him even more tightly—and found himself slipping, rolling off the couch to land flat on his back on the floor. Mandy clapped a hand to her mouth, holding in shocked laughter. "Oh, Kevin, I'm so sorry! Are you all right?"

He laughed right back up at her, then reached and tugged until she slithered off the couch to stretch out on top of him. He laced his hands through her hair and pulled her down for another hot, wet kiss.

119

Finally, they had to come up for air. He leaned his forehead against hers. "Mandy. Ask me to stay."

Chapter Thirteen

Mandy eased out from under the covers and padded around the end of the bed to turn off her alarm before it buzzed and woke Kevin. Grabbing clean clothes for the day, she headed into the bathroom for a quick shower.

He was still sleeping when she popped back in: sprawled on his belly, face buried in the pillow. She unplugged her phone and stuffed it in her pocket, then leaned over him to pull the blanket back up over his shoulder. He lifted his head and opened one eye, glanced at the clock, and rolled over, tugging her down onto him. "Morning. You're up early." His voice was muffled at the side of her neck.

"Late for me. We don't open till eight on Sundays so I don't have to be down there till six."

"Mmm. You smell good. And it's not six yet. Come back to bed?"

She suppressed a giggle as he snuffled into her hair. It tickled. "I can't. No, really, Kevin," she protested, her voice somewhere between a laugh and a sigh. "I need to go."

She sat up, reluctantly, her hands on his chest. Fine brown hair arrowed down his belly and continued down under the sheet barely covering one of his best features, the one currently nudging her in the side.

As tired as she felt, she heated up fast at his touch. They'd made love a number of times since returning to her apartment. At one point, he'd gone out to the kitchen and retrieved the rest of the homemade truffles and ice wine. Little paper cups from the desserts and the occasional empty condom wrapper littered her bedroom. Later they'd grabbed a quick shower together to wash off the remains of the chocolate.

But playtime was over, at least for the morning, and she had to get to work. "Go back to sleep. Just because I have to be up doesn't mean you have to." Mandy leaned down to kiss him softly. "Make sure the door locks behind you when you leave, okay?"

Kevin reached up and cupped the back of her head, bringing her down for another, more thorough kiss. "What time do you close today?" he murmured against her mouth.

"Um. Usually between six and seven on a Sunday. Depends on—"

"I know. It depends on when you run out of cupcakes." He shook his head, bemused. "I'm still trying to figure out how you can run a business on those terms."

Mandy stood up, breaking free from his loose grasp. "Well, maybe it wouldn't work in a big city like Calgary. But it works fine in Harmony." She turned and headed for the door. "One more reason I like it here. I can be more flexible."

"Yeah?" he asked, settling back on the pillows again. "Flexible enough to have dinner with me again?"

"Kevin…"

"Mandy… Seriously. Have dinner with me tonight."

"Not tonight. I have dinner with Auntie Anna on Sunday nights."

"Tomorrow, then. Or Tuesday. Or Wednesday. Whatever works for you."

She ducked her head and gave him a quick nod, saying, "Okay. Choose a day this week, and call me."

* * *

"You know I love your cupcake of the month idea, but by the third week I get really tired of making so many of the same flavor. I can smell the peppermint icing from the parking lot."

Mandy slid another full tray of cupcakes into the rack as Kelsey came in through the side door. "You'll be glad to know I've got enough of them here for most of the day. You can start on the regular flavors." She pushed the rolling rack over to the walk-in fridge. "There. You won't smell them as much now."

"Except for this batch—you want these in the case up front?" Kelsey's voice sounded muffled as she pulled off her coat and hung it in Mandy's office. She came back to wash her hands, then studied their big whiteboard to check the schedule. "Mmmm. Chocolate with salted caramel icing. My favorite."

"You and Auntie Anna both. First four batches of cupcakes are cooling in the walk-in. Why don't you get your favorite frosting going? I'll take these out front."

As she walked the remaining tray through the doors to the shop in front, she heard Kelsey call, "Then you can come back here and tell me all about your dinner last night!"

Well, crap. Should never have let her trade her day off with Zak. Not for today. Mandy took her time placing the freshly iced cupcakes into the display cases. When she couldn't stall any longer, she heaved a big sigh and headed back into the kitchen to face her friend's questions.

"So? Spill!" Kelsey laughed as she took the pot containing the frosting base off the stove burner and moved to the big stand mixer at the worktable. "You look a little, I don't know, stunned, maybe? You had either a really good time or a really bad time. Which was it?"

"Not stunned. Tired." Mandy brushed by her friend and started gathering ingredients for her own favorite frosting, chocolate cream cheese.

"Oh, yeah? What time did you roll in? And speak up; I'm about to turn this beast on."

With her back to the room, Mandy rolled her eyes. No use procrastinating. She'd never been able to keep anything from Kelsey, so why should today be any different? "We got back here around midnight. And before you get your knickers in a knot, yes, I said *we*. Kevin helped me bring all the equipment and stuff back."

"Oh, did he, now? And then what, you sent him back to his lonely hotel room?"

Mandy dropped her load of ingredients on the table and started unwrapping pounds of butter and sorting them into the various mixing bowls. "Not exactly."

Kelsey turned off the stand mixer, scraped down the sides of the bowl, and transferred the frosting into a piping bag. "Not exactly? What does— Wait. What's that noise?"

They heard the sounds of a door closing overhead, followed by footsteps and a cheerful whistle descending the stairs from the apartment above. Mandy held her breath until the outer door opened and closed, then let it out with a rush.

Kelsey threw her a look that said *You have got to be kidding me!*, grabbed Mandy by the hand, and dragged her into the front of the shop. Together they watched Kevin saunter across the street and head down the block to the Thurston Hotel.

"Holy crap. You slept with him!"

The curse of the fair-skinned, the blush swept up from the middle of her chest and up into her hairline. "I might have."

"You might have? Oh, girl, you so did!" Kelsey whooped and laughed so hard tears ran down her cheeks. "I can't believe you did that. You, who barely ever dates, who hasn't been with a guy in over a year, you slept with a guy on the first date."

"Technically it wasn't a date," Mandy replied carefully. "Technically I worked for him last night."

"And it gets better and better. So you slept with him *before* your first date." Kelsey shook her head, and mock-

125

bowed to her. "Oh, grasshopper. You have learned your lesson well. I am so proud."

"No! Not before the first date. There will be no first date, or second date, for that matter. We're not dating. Besides," she countered, "weren't you the one who thought this would be a good idea?"

"It is a good idea! Get him hooked on your food, get him into bed, get him convinced to not want to buy your land and tear down your building."

"Jeez, Kels, it wasn't anything like that. It just... happened. I didn't plan anything. We finished dinner, he offered to help me get all the equipment back here, and then, well, we'd had a lot of wine, and one thing led to another."

"So you really did sleep with him on a whim?"

Mandy shrugged. "I guess. I certainly didn't think it through last night."

She thought about it now, though. She thought through Kelsey's continuing to tease her right up until they opened, through Suzette coming in to help with the Sunday morning after-church rush and her teasing, and all the way through the day, till she found herself alone at dusk in the front of the shop, wiping out the inside of her now-empty display cases.

The bells jingled as the door opened. Mandy spoke before she looked up. "I'm sorry, we're sold out for the day. Do you want to place an order— Oh, hi, Auntie Anna. I didn't know you'd be stopping in. Aren't I supposed to come by your place for dinner later?" She came around the counter to kiss her great-aunt hello.

"Hello, dear. Yes, and I already have a nice stew cooking in the crock pot. My book club ran a little late at the Margaret Library, so I thought I'd pop in and keep you company until you're ready to go."

"Mrs. Lipiczki, nice to see you!" Kelsey came out from the back, wiping her hands on a towel, and greeted the older woman with a smile and a hug.

"And how are those babies of yours doing, hmm? I thought you stayed home with them and your charming husband on weekends."

"I usually do. I traded my days off this weekend with Zak for his Thursday and Friday. Brian and I are going up to Edmonton next weekend to bring the babies to see his grandmother, and I wanted a couple of extra days. Besides, this way I got to hear all about Mandy's special dinner with Kevin MacNeal last night. Before she forgot any of the juicy details." She ignored Mandy's frantic signaling and winked at Anna. "You should ask her how it went."

"Oh, I've already heard all about it. He's been singing her praises all day over at the Thurston Hotel. Couldn't say enough nice things about the dinner, how wonderful everything tasted, and how smoothly everything went."

She turned to her great-niece. "I know you don't think much of his development plan for Main Street, Mandy. But he really is a very nice young man. You should go out with him; you two would make a lovely couple."

"What, are you matchmaking for me now? Auntie Anna, you do know he lives in Calgary, right?" Mandy shook her head. She locked the front door and herded the two of them into the back before her, shutting off lights as she went. "Come on, let's get going."

Chapter Fourteen

Kevin took off his coat and shook the rain from it, trying to keep the runoff confined to the big mat by the heavy front doors. He'd learned the hard way how slick the marble floors of the Thurston Hotel got when they were wet. He now kept a pair of shoes in his truck, so he could sit on the bench inside the door and swap his muddy boots for clean (well, cleaner) footwear. The surface of the ground was starting to thaw in the milder temperatures of late March, and spring thaws meant mud. Lots of it.

Grabbing his boots by the laces, he stood to head for the elevator, just as Mandy barreled in through the door and right into his arms. He managed to keep his grip on both the boots and the girl, but he couldn't stop the transfer of some mud from one to the other. "Oh, jeez, Mandy, I'm sorry!"

"No harm done. I'm already wet and filthy." She pulled her soaking jeans away from her leg and made a face. "You can't have made them any worse than they already are."

He eyed her, torn between laughter and sympathy. Her jeans really were in worse shape than his boots. "What happened to you?"

"Flat tire on Auntie Anna's car. I had the spare swapped on and the old one in the trunk when some bozo went by and splashed me. I think he actually swerved to go through the biggest part of the puddle. Idiot."

She grabbed the bottom of her coat and squeezed. Cold, muddy water ran down over her hands onto the mat. "What a mess. Look, I've got to go outside and wring this out a bit. Could you do me a favor? I'm here to pick up my great-aunt and Emily Jamieson. They had tea with Mrs. A in the Margaret Library this afternoon. Would you go in there and let them know I'm here, and I'll go outside and see if I can get rid of some of this water?"

"Sure." He turned toward the lobby, then turned back. "Why didn't you call someone to change the flat? Actually, why didn't your great-aunt call somebody to change the flat?"

"She did. She called me." Mandy cocked her head to one side. "Who else would she have called?"

"I don't know, the automobile association? A local garage?"

She snorted with amusement. "This isn't the big city. We save our emergency calls for emergencies. I can change a tire as well as those guys. Why should she pay for someone to come out when I can do it for her?"

"What would she do if you weren't here? Or you couldn't come right away?"

"Well, then, she'd have to call someone else, wouldn't she? But I am here, and available, and if the jerk with the pickup hadn't gotten his jollies by splashing me, I wouldn't even be this wet and grubby." She sighed and pushed a lock of hair away from her eyes where it had fallen out of the clip holding the blonde mass back. "But I am wet, and grubby, and cold. So if you wouldn't mind…?"

"Of course. Sorry. I'll be right back with them."

Who knew it would take so long to herd the two old ladies out of the library? Finally, he had them both moving in the same direction at the same time, with Mrs. A trailing behind on her way somewhere, back up to her suite, he supposed.

Instead, she followed them through the lobby to where Mandy waited by the door. He could see her shivering from across the room. When they got closer, her blue lips indicated how chilled she'd gotten.

"Mandy, what happened?" Anna hurried over to her great-niece and reached for her hands, rubbing them between her own to warm them.

"Got splashed while I changed your flat," Mandy explained through chattering teeth. "Are you two ready to go? I—"

"Why didn't you go home and change before coming to get me? Or I could have called a cab to take us home."

"Because I didn't. Can we go now? My van's out front and I can't leave it there much longer." She turned for the door.

"Your van? Did you leave my car at the bank? I don't suppose they'll mind if I leave it in their parking lot overnight." Anna bit her lip.

"No, I drove it to your place. Your tire's in the back of my van. Tomorrow I'll run it over to the dealership and get a new tire mounted on the rim. I don't know whether they've got one in stock, and I didn't want you to worry about your car over at the bank. I walked back to get my van, which is why I'm so cold. I'll take you home, then—"

"Don't be silly," interrupted Kevin. "Go home, take a hot shower, and get into some dry clothes." He turned to Anna and her friend. "Why don't I drive the two of you home?"

"Oh, how nice of you! If you're sure it's not too much trouble?"

"Not at all." He sat down to swap his footwear again. "I've got this covered, Mandy, if you want to go home and get warm?"

Mandy gave him a doubtful look. "You don't have to."

"No, I don't, but I will. And the longer you stand here, the colder you get." He stood, boots on, ready to go. "I'll walk out with you and bring my car around. All right, Mrs. Lipiczki, Mrs. Jamieson? Wait here so you don't have to walk so far in the rain."

He took Mandy's elbow, nudging her out the door before she had a chance to object. He steered her over to her waiting van, then trotted out into the lot to fetch his own car once she had driven off.

With the seniors in his car, Kevin drove a little slower and a little more carefully than he might have on his own. The short drive didn't give them a lot of time to pump him for information, but they did their best.

"You live in Calgary, don't you? Do you have family there?" Emily leaned forward and tapped his shoulder. "Will you be here until the town hall and community center are all done?"

"Emily, give the man a chance to answer!" scolded Anna.

Kevin chuckled. "That's okay. The answers are yes, no, and yes. Yes, I live in Calgary. No, I don't have any family there. My folks sold their farm and retired to Arizona last year. And yes, I'm here till the town hall and community center are done."

"Which might be for months and months, right?"

"That's right. We're working on getting the site ready at the moment, and we break ground on the new construction next month." Everybody knew the timing. What was their point?

"Is there anyone special waiting for you back in Calgary?"

And there came the real reason behind the questions. "Ah, no."

"Emily, enough! Don't badger the man. Besides, we're here."

Kevin pulled up in front of the covered entrance and walked around to help both women out of the car. Emily thanked him for the ride and headed into the building.

Anna hung back a little. "Would you like to come inside? We always have coffee and tea and treats in the common room."

133

Here he'd been racking his brain trying to think of a way to talk to her privately about the land, and she handed it to him on a silver platter. "Sure. Let me park the car—you have a visitor's spot, right?" He parked where she indicated and followed her into the building.

At his nod, Anna poured them both coffee and led him over to some comfy chairs flanking a fireplace. "Now, what's this I hear about you and my great-niece?"

Kevin sputtered on his coffee. He knew a trick question when he heard one. How could he answer without getting himself in hot water?

Anna raised her eyebrows. "I meant that to be a relatively innocuous question. Now you make me wonder what question I should really ask you."

"Why don't we start with your innocuous one?" He dabbed at his chin with the napkin she handed him.

"Hmm. I suppose I can always ask Mandy herself." She took a sip, keeping her level gaze on his over the rim of her cup. "What I wanted to talk to you about is why Brock Anderson has tried for the past two weeks to set up a meeting between us."

"Oh, that." He was disappointed. Why was he disappointed? He should be relieved she only wanted to talk about business. Not his upcoming date with Mandy. Not the fundraiser entry for which he had entered an outrageous bid on a whim. Not the fabulous dinner Mandy had made for him because of his bid. And certainly not the amazing night he'd spent in her bed afterwards. No, he certainly didn't want to talk about any of those.

Back to business. This might be his only chance to plant a seed in Anna Lipiczki's mind, one that could result in his acquiring the property for his investors. "I wanted to talk about purchasing a parcel of land on Main Street, but he stayed very close-mouthed about who actually owns it."

"I see. And by now I'm sure you have figured out who the owners are?"

Kevin nodded. "I've known for some time the Schmidt Family Corporation owns the land. But I couldn't find any Schmidts in Harmony anymore."

"That's because my father only had daughters. My sister didn't want any part of the family business. The family of the man she married was ashamed their son married a baker's daughter, so my husband Joe and I bought out her share, shortly after we married. She moved away to Calgary. I don't see her very often anymore." Anna sniffed in disdain. "Too bad for them. Joe and I did just fine."

She looked at him, considering. "Has Mandy said anything about her parents?"

"A little. I know her father was never part of the picture, and her mother was…"

"Her mother was an irresponsible brat who got herself pregnant at sixteen, which appalled my brother-in-law's relations even more than him having married into a family of bakers. When they tossed her out, I took her in." She sighed. "The only good thing Janine ever did was to have that sweet girl."

"And they traveled around a lot when Mandy was young," he prompted.

"Until she turned eighteen and put a stop to it. She went to baking arts school in Calgary, of course, but she's lived in Harmony ever since."

"So you and your husband gave her a leg up in the baking business?" Did gratitude keep Mandy here?

"She came to work for us, yes. But she took over when Joe retired, then bought me out when he died, and started Whimsy herself. She and I jointly own the land and the building, but she is the sole owner of Whimsy." Anna tipped her head in puzzlement. "You could have gotten most of that from the corporate registry, you know, all the ownership details anyway."

"But not the reasons why. Personal details don't show on land titles or incorporation papers." Kevin set down his cup. "I'm trying to figure out why your great-niece is so against selling."

Her spoon made a rasping sound as she stirred her coffee. "Have you asked her?"

"Sort of. But her answer doesn't make sense to me. She talks about wanting to stay in Harmony but never explains why. I know she wants to expand into a café. I'm trying to figure out why she doesn't want to expand by moving into a bigger market."

Anna put her cup down. "You know, sometimes things, people, really are as they seem. Mandy is happy here. She chose to come back and live here, even after her training. She wants her business to grow, yes, but she wants to do it here. And I know she loves to cook, not only bake. So why not expand here?"

"Because—"

"Hold on, young man. I'm not done," she admonished. "There's also the risk factor. If Mandy relocated Whimsy to Calgary, she'd be starting from scratch again. New market, new competitors, no local support system. By expanding here, even though she'll be opening a new and different kind of business, she's doing it someplace familiar. She has friends here. She knows the market, and she knows her potential employees. Mandy generally doesn't do things on a whim. She's not really a risk-taker, for all that she's an entrepreneur."

Her reason made more sense to Kevin than he wanted to admit. He could relate to not wanting to take a risk. Hadn't he faced the same sort of decision when he chose to work for his current firm instead of striking out on his own? He didn't usually do things on a whim, either.

But what was Saturday night, then, if not a whim? For both of them?

He stopped his train of thought in its tracks and focused on the woman in front of him instead of the one in his head. "But sometimes taking a risk is the right thing to do. And what about you?"

"Me? This doesn't have anything to do with me, other than that since we are the only partners in the Schmidt Family Corporation we both have to agree in order to sell the land."

"But it does have to do with you." Kevin leaned forward to drive his point home. "One of the reasons Mandy feels tied to Harmony is her tie to you. She feels responsible for you, even if she doesn't live with you. You called her to take care of your flat tire, right? And she left the shop to come and deal with it."

"What's your point, Mr. MacNeal?"

Don't piss off the great-aunt. Whatever you do, don't piss off the great-aunt. You need her on your side. "In a bigger city like Calgary, wouldn't you have access to more services and better care? Mandy wouldn't have to worry about you so much, or come running when you needed help. She'd be able to focus more on the business—and on her own life."

"On her own life? Are you saying she's focused on my life and not her own?"

Anna's expression settled somewhere between insulted and appalled. Kevin figured he better tread a little more softly. "Well, maybe not exclusively. But she does worry about you, doesn't she? And you've commented to more than one person you're worried she's so wrapped up in Whimsy she doesn't have much of a personal life."

"Wherever did you hear something like that?"

"As I've been told over and over again, Harmony's a small town. Everyone knows everyone. It's no secret Mandy doesn't date, and she spends most of her time at the shop. Starting a second business here will keep her tied to the business, and tied to the town, even aside from her ties to you."

"I can't tell her what to do with her business. Whimsy is all hers." Anna paled a little, but she still listened. "But there may be something to what you're saying, about her feeling tied to the town because I'm here. Are you suggesting I tell her she shouldn't worry about me?"

Time for a strategic retreat. "I'm not suggesting you tell her that, no. She's always going to feel she owes you a lot. You raised her, you stepped in to fill the gap her mother couldn't. But I'm suggesting—no, I'm asking—for you to keep an open mind on the land deal. Maybe encourage her to do some looking around in Calgary, for Whimsy's sake. If the two of you agreed to sell the land, you'd be set for life. You could hire whatever help you needed, move into a place with a higher level of care when the time comes. And Mandy could take the money from the sale of the land to move or expand or do whatever she wants with the business."

"Honestly, I'm less concerned about her business than about her personal life. I don't want her to feel like she has to take care of me. And you're right; she doesn't date because she's always at the shop. And because"—she wrinkled her nose—"partly because I don't think she's ever found anyone here she's interested in."

Then she surprised him. "And what about you, Mr. MacNeal? You've been here in Harmony for a few months now, and you'll be here at least a few months longer. Don't you miss your own personal life?"

Crap. Small towns. Everybody knows everything. Surely Mandy hadn't told her great-aunt they had spent Saturday night together? Before he could formulate a coherent answer, she continued, "It's clear your interest in Mandy goes beyond your interest in her land. It's also clear she feels... Well, I don't know what she feels. You make her uncomfortable, which is not necessarily a bad thing. It would be good for my girl to move out of her comfort zone a little bit. And you might be the man to get her there."

Anna rose from her chair, waited for him to pick up his coat, and walked him to the door. "I'll make you a deal, Mr. MacNeal: I'll listen to what you have to say, but I won't try to influence her either way about the land. Or about you."

Then she gave him a look, one reminiscent of the look his mother gave him as a kid when she knew he and his friends were up to some mischief. "Unless you break her heart. Then all bets are off."

Chapter Fifteen

Mandy settled on her couch next to Kevin. Over the last week, they'd alternated between his hotel room and her apartment. Sometimes they had dinner together, sometimes not, depending on whether one or the other one was working late. Or in Kevin's case, playing hockey in the men's league at the old rec center. But they'd managed to spend a chunk of each evening—and most of the nights—together.

She smiled into her coffee as his arm settled around her shoulders. She appreciated having someone to talk to about her day, someone who hadn't spent the entire day locked in a hot kitchen with her as they scrambled to fill orders.

At her sigh, he asked, "Something wrong?"

"No, just thinking. I really need to find at least one more full-time employee for Whimsy. Maybe two. The specialty cake side is taking off, and I want to focus on getting it well established before I expand."

He played with the ends of her hair. "Do you have a timetable?"

"I wish. It depends entirely on when Connie decides to retire."

"You mentioned that. Would you combine the spaces? Won't that be hard, in an older building? You can't blindly knock walls down. I've seen where the support beams are in the basement."

"I wouldn't have to. I'd expand up instead of sideways. This apartment, right above Whimsy, I'd turn into the kitchen for the café and eventually the catering side. When I did the reno and expansion downstairs, I had them run new electrical and higher-capacity ventilation up here too. And they reinforced the floor to take the extra weight of commercial equipment."

"So the café next door will be only on the main floor?"

"And a second room above it, for overflow seating if we get busy, private functions, that sort of thing. I'd change the hallway and stairs between the two spaces so it all works better. I wont have to knock any walls down."

"If you turn this apartment into a kitchen for the café, where will you live?"

"The other two apartments in this block are empty. I could move into one of those." Mandy sipped her coffee. "If I could find an employee for Whimsy willing to take the early-morning shift, maybe I'd buy a house in one of the new developments on the edge of town."

Kevin took her empty coffee cup and put it with his own on the low table in front of them. "You've put a lot of thought into this. But if you're having trouble finding employees for the bakery side, is it smart to expand into a café too?"

She laughed. "It's actually easier to find café employees. The hours are shorter, and even the breakfast shift would start later than I do now. And most of the positions don't need as much specialty experience. If I want a baker, I may have to recruit outside of Harmony. But line cooks and servers I can probably find."

"You don't think it would be easier to build and expand in Calgary?"

"Nah. My friends and instructors from pastry chef school talk about the high turnover rates in restaurants and bakeries there. Here, when someone finds a job, they settle in for a while. There's a lot of stability in a small town you don't get in a bigger city."

"I'll have to take your word on that." He buried his face in her hair. "But not right now."

"No?" She twisted around to drape her legs over his. "Had something different in mind?" she asked, winding her arms around his neck.

He brushed her lips with his, gently first, then pressed more firmly. "I don't want to talk about business right now." He shifted fast, pulling her all the way onto his lap. "I want to talk about something else."

"Talk?" she teased. "You want to talk?" She nuzzled at his jaw. "Are you sure about that?"

Kevin groaned, then leaned his head away from her, barely enough so she couldn't reach to kiss him. He traced her smiling mouth with the tip of his finger, then nipped her bottom lip. "I want to have dinner with you."

"Tomorrow? Sure. I'll cook if you shop. Your place or mine?"

"No, I mean take you to dinner. A date. In a restaurant. Where all of Harmony can see."

Her heart gave a lurch, then settled back into its steady beat, but in a faster rhythm. *It's a date. Not a long-term commitment.* "You want to date? Like, really date?"

"Yes, I want to really date. We've been spending a lot of time together." He grinned. "I've had more than one person ask me what my intentions are."

"Oh, man." She buried her face in his shoulder and shook with laughter. "Seriously?"

"Yep. Apparently the good citizens of Harmony feel obliged to stick their collective noses into our business."

"Welcome to small-town Alberta." Mandy giggled at his expression.

"Since we started out by not hitting it off, I think they want to make sure we're not constantly sniping at each other. Or they really have nothing better to do than to pry into our personal lives. What do you say? Want to satisfy their curiosity and appear in public together?"

He was serious, she realized. Both about dating her, and about appeasing the town's inquisitive minds. And maybe, just maybe, this might be about more than her land. Maybe this was about her.

"I would like that, very much." She hesitated, then added, "You do realize in a restaurant, we're fair game for anybody and everybody to come and talk to, right?"

"Hmm."

Mandy grinned. Maybe she was getting through to him. Maybe the big-city boy could grow into a small-town man after all.

Chapter Sixteen

Kevin leaned on the back of his chair in the Foothills Dining Room, the upscale restaurant in the Thurston Hotel, talking to Brock. They watched Riley and Mandy, deep into discussions about Riley's wedding cake. Between the distance and the background noise, Kevin figured they wouldn't be overheard if they kept their voices down.

At least he and Mandy had finally been able to finish their main course without interruptions. It seemed like every time there had been a lull in their meal, someone—or several someones—had taken the opportunity to come over and chat. Even as he watched, Mrs. A joined in the women's conversation.

"Is it always like this?" he asked Brock quietly.

"What, getting your date interrupted by the friendly citizens of Harmony? Yeah, pretty much. Remember, you're a newbie here: someone they don't know anything about. And Mandy works long hours and doesn't socialize much. Seeing her out on a date is as much a novelty as having you in town. So, sure, everyone's curious. Especially since the two of you got off to a rocky start at the Chamber meeting." He looked sideways at Kevin. "This is a date, right? Not a business meeting?"

"Yes, it's a date. It feels weird having to share the evening with the town, though."

"Welcome to Harmony, where your business is our business." Brock chuckled, then laughed outright at Kevin's glum expression.

"Business? Oh, this is a business discussion? I'm surprised at you, Brock Anderson," scolded Mrs. A, turning to them. "Wasting a Saturday night out with your honey on business. Don't you have regular office hours? And you," she continued, turning on Kevin. "I had better hopes for you, young man."

"Me? What did I do?"

"Oh, come now. Everyone knows you're trying to buy Mandy's land. Why, the other day—"

"Wait. Wait. What do you mean, everyone knows I'm trying to buy her land?" He rounded on Brock, who threw up his hands and shook his head.

"Don't look at me. I haven't told anyone anything." Brock looked at his fiancée. "Riley?"

"Not me either." She put her arm around a visibly upset Mandy.

"Oh, don't be silly. Of course neither one of them would ever talk about a client's business. But Anna Lipiczki is a dear friend of mine, and we talk. So I know, Mr. MacNeal, about the discussion the two of you had earlier this week. Which is why," she said, "I thought this might be a business discussion. You know, to talk about the land deal."

Kevin's stomach felt like it dropped somewhere to the vicinity of his shoes. He looked at Mrs. A in horror as she

146

addressed Mandy, "Honey, you don't have to sell, you know. Anna said—"

"Mrs. A, MRS. A!" Mandy raised her voice to be heard over the older woman. "Hang on a sec."

She turned slowly to face him. "Did you talk to my great-aunt about buying the land?"

"Well, yes, but—"

She held up her hand. "Stop." She turned to Brock. "Did you know he spoke to my great-aunt?"

"Not… exactly. No. He asked for a meeting with the directors of the Schmidt Family Corporation, I spoke to you, you said you weren't interested in selling, and I told him no meeting. And he didn't hear from me Anna Lipiczki was the other partner."

"Mandy, look, it wasn't—"

"Not ready to talk to you yet." Mandy closed her eyes and took a deep breath, then said to Mrs. A, "What, exactly, did my great-aunt say to you, about this meeting she had with Kevin about the land? No, wait, first things first. When did they have this meeting?"

"It wasn't a meeting! It—"

"Still not ready to talk to you," she cut Kevin off again. "Mrs. A?"

"Oh, honey, he's right. It wasn't like he set up a meeting or anything. He didn't go through Anderson & Anderson. He didn't have to! But when he drove her home the other night, when she had the flat tire? Well, I guess he couldn't pass up the opportunity. They talked then."

"I see."

Kevin could almost see the wheels turning as Mandy weighed that piece of information. And he was pretty sure the result wouldn't be in his favor.

"All right, Kevin, your turn. What exactly did you and my great-aunt talk about when you drove her home? No, wait, first tell me how you managed to talk about anything as serious as this land deal in the two-minute drive between the Thurston Hotel and the Residence at Pineview."

"You're right, we didn't talk on the ride. For one thing, Mrs. Jamieson rode with us, remember? Your great-aunt invited me in afterward and we had a cup of coffee in the common room."

Her face, already pale, went even whiter. "She invited you in for coffee and cookies? And you pressured her about selling out? Not a very nice way to repay someone's hospitality, is it?"

"It wasn't like that! I didn't pressure her. I merely asked her to consider the proposal. Brock had spoken to her about meeting regarding the sale, and she wanted to know why."

Brock stepped back. "Don't put me in the middle of this. Look at the timing, Mandy. Once you said no sale, I stopped asking your great-aunt for a meeting, you know that."

"I know this has nothing to do with you, Brock, and everything to do with Kevin." She turned back to him. "Doesn't it?"

"Hey, look, I didn't offer to drive her home so I could grill her about your family business! In fact, she had questions for me. She wanted to know…" *Uh oh. Didn't really want to start down this path.*

"She wanted to know what?"

Kevin took a deep breath. "We talked about you, mostly. I think she wanted to know what my intentions were. Are. And then one thing led to another, and then we were talking about the land, and I—"

"So, you were talking about me, which led right to a discussion about the land?"

The more upset she got, the louder her voice got. They were starting to draw attention from surrounding tables. He had to nip this in the bud.

"Look, can we talk about this some other time? And some other place? People are watching."

"Good! Let them watch. Let them hear. I want to hear too."

"So do I."

Kevin could only describe the voice as smarmy. Or slimy. That had been his impression of the editor of the local paper from the first time they'd met, when the town had announced who won the design bid for the municipal projects, and the paper had interviewed him. Aaron Bridges had been an example of the worst sort of small-town inhabitant. Exhibiting more than the normal nosiness Kevin had come to expect from Harmony's residents, Bridges always slanted his stories to show the nastier side of people.

"Get lost, Bridges. This is a private conversation," growled Brock.

"In a public restaurant? I don't think so. Besides, this is news. All of Harmony wants to know if the Main Street redevelopment is a go. And since the biggest obstacle is the current landowner, anything she has to say on the matter is fair game. So what is it, Ms. Brighton?" he asked. "Is he after your land? Or after you? Want to make a statement for the *Chronicle*?"

Bridges aimed his cell phone in her direction to record her reaction. Kevin lunged for it. Brock held him back, saying softly, "Don't react. Don't give him a reason to claim you're obstructing him. Besides, Mandy can take care of herself."

"If you had asked me what his interest in me was an hour ago," Mandy said, her voice strained, "you might have gotten a different answer. Now? It doesn't matter. You want a statement for the paper? I'll give you a statement. The Schmidt Family Corporation is not in negotiations to sell our land along Main Street. We do not intend to sell. Not now, not ever. It's my family legacy. It's part of Harmony's history. Whimsy and I are staying put."

She whirled on Kevin. "As for you? Stay away from my great-aunt. Stay away from my land. Stay away from me. Anything else you want to say to me, say it to my lawyer." She pointed at Brock, then picked up her evening bag and coat and headed for the door.

"Mandy—"

"No. Don't say it. You've said enough."

Chapter Seventeen

On Sunday, she'd been numb. The pain seemed remote, as if it had happened to someone else. The incident replayed in her mind like watching TV with the sound off. She knew what happened, but it didn't—quite—get through to her. She'd even been able to serve Whimsy's customers in the morning before Zak came in and took over the front of the shop. Long-standing habits meant everything got done, and done well, even if she didn't remember doing them.

On Monday, she'd been upset. Every cut, every sting, felt as fresh and painful as it had Saturday night. Her red eyes and sniffles kept her confined to the kitchen. Once Suzette came in after school, Mandy had found any number of reasons to stay in her office: doing her books, ordering supplies, and reviewing the résumés of potential employees while repeatedly having to take time out to dry her eyes and blow her nose.

By the time Kelsey came back to work Tuesday morning, Mandy was angry. Deep down, to-the-bone angry.

There had been no word from Kevin since Saturday night. Or none she knew of, anyway. She let someone else get Whimsy's phone each time it rang, and only a few calls had come to her cell (from her great-aunt, from Riley, and finally one from Kelsey when she'd gotten back into town last night). If he had called the shop or stopped in, no one told her.

Which was probably for the better, she thought grimly as she kneaded a batch of fondant to mix in the color. Yesterday she'd have cried all over him, but today she'd be more likely to throw something at him.

"I think that batch is mixed enough. Want to move on to something different?"

Mandy looked up at Kelsey. "Sure. Too bad we don't have any yeast on hand. Punching down bread dough for cinnamon buns would feel good right about now."

"Not exactly what I had in mind, although cinnamon buns would be awesome and we should totally get some yeast. Want to talk about what happened Saturday night?"

"I guess it was too much to hope for that you hadn't heard about it just because you were out of town." Mandy wrapped the fondant in cling wrap and went over to the utility sink to wash off the sticky residue.

She didn't like the sound of the silence behind her. Turning as she dried her hands, she caught Kelsey looking anywhere but at her.

Tossing the paper towel in the trash, Mandy returned to the worktable. "Spill."

"Isn't that supposed to be my line?"

"You first. Unlike most of Harmony, you weren't in the restaurant when I had my meltdown in public. In fact, you didn't even get back into town till last night, and I didn't mention it when you called. So how did you hear?"

If she hadn't been watching closely, she never would have noticed Kelsey's quick glance toward the door. "What?

Did Zak tell you? No, it couldn't have been him. You came in through the back this morning, and you haven't been out front yet. You haven't even spoken to him, I don't think. So who?"

"You haven't been on social media since Saturday, have you?"

Oh, no. No, no, no. "Don't tell me Arrogant Aaron posted about what happened."

Kelsey slid off her stool and went to Mandy's office. She came back into the kitchen and handed over her iPad, the *Chronicle*'s Facebook page already loaded up. "Here. You'd better read it yourself."

Bridges had written it like an article, headline and all. "Local Landowner Stops Development: Can Harmony Afford to Live in the Past?"

Her ears burned as she clicked on the "See more" link to read the rest. Hell, her whole face burned. She was surprised the iPad hadn't self-combusted or melted in her hands by the time she finished reading the whole post.

Apparently she should feel single-handedly responsible for an impending economic downturn. Her refusal to sell her land would bring development to a screeching halt and scare off any potential investors anywhere in the town. And reading between the lines, it seemed no one in Harmony but her thought Kevin's interest in her could have been for any reason other than a stupid land deal.

She thought about punching down cinnamon rolls again, and a memory of kneading bread dough on this very worktable with her Uncle Joe flashed through her mind. She'd been no more than four or five, and had to kneel on the stool to reach. She glanced over to the double doors leading to the front of the shop, finding her height growth lines he had measured and marked every time she stayed with them. No way she would ever sell this place. How could she leave her memories behind?

She didn't realize the tears were falling until Kelsey took the iPad from her shaking fingers and replaced it with a box of tissues. "Here, hon. Take a minute, then tell me what's going on."

Mandy wiped away the tears, tossed the tissue, and faced her friend. "Nothing. Nothing's going on. Even though I thought something might be going on, it's not. It was always about the land. It was never about me."

"I'm not so sure. Have you seen the way he looks at you? You can't tell me there isn't... something... there."

Mandy laughed bitterly. "Oh, I'm sure there was. It's a nice fringe benefit, isn't it, if you get to sleep with your opponent? Makes it all the sweeter when you win the land deal, if you also win the girl."

"Oh, Mandy, I'm sure it wasn't only about the land."

"Are you? I'm not. How can I be? Kelsey, he's wined and dined me for almost two weeks now. We've spent almost every night together, sometimes here and sometimes at his place." She shook her head. "I thought we really had something."

"I know. I watched you. You've been on more dates with him in the last two weeks than I think you have in all the years I've worked for you." Kelsey put her arm around Mandy's shoulders and squeezed. "You were falling for him, weren't you?"

"I suppose. But who did I fall for, Kels? I thought he was this great guy, someone who wanted me for me, not for my land. I probably should have seen it coming. After that first night? We never talked about the land or the development or even about his business in Harmony. Even though Whimsy is so important to me, and building and development is so important to him, we never talked about it."

"He broke your heart."

"No. Dented it a little, maybe. But things hadn't gotten serious yet. We were taking it slow. Or I thought so, anyway. I didn't want to get involved with someone who'd be leaving in a few months." Mandy shrugged helplessly. "Maybe I read too much into the fact we didn't talk. Maybe I thought since he never actually came out and asked me to sell, and he stopped asking Brock to set up meetings between us, he'd changed his mind. But going behind my back to Auntie Anna, well, that's when I—"

"Wait, wait! He did what? He talked to your great-aunt about selling the land? When did he do such a thing? How could he do such a thing? Has he no scruples at all? What's wrong with that man?"

Kelsey stomped around their kitchen in full tirade mode. Zak stuck his head through the swinging doors, took one look, and slowly backed out of the room again without saying a word.

If it didn't hurt so much, it would be funny. Kelsey was a spitfire when she was mad. Her rubber-soled shoes were silent on the tile floor, so she pushed into stools and banged steel bowls and generally made as much noise as she could without screaming.

Finally, she came to a stop next to Mandy. "What. Did. He. Do?"

"I don't know, exactly. Auntie Anna hasn't said. And I haven't spoken to him since Saturday."

"I don't blame you for not taking his calls. He—"

"No. He hasn't called. Or stopped in the shop."

Kelsey's eyes widened. "What do you mean, he hasn't called? He hasn't apologized? He should be in here groveling! What is wrong with him?" She sat down with a huff. "No wonder you're mad."

The tears were giving way to anger again, which was good. It was great. "Better to be angry at a sneaky, slimy wheeler and dealer who's trying to get me to give up my land and move away from my home than to cry over a guy who broke my heart. He's not worth it."

"I should say not!" Kelsey sprang up again. "So what are you going to do about it?"

"Do? Nothing. What can I do about someone who doesn't really want me, except get over him?"

"And is that what you want? To get over him?"

Mandy stared at her friend. "Ten seconds ago he was the scum of the earth. Now you're asking me whether or not I want to get over him?"

"Yes. This is all about you. If you want him, we need to fix this." Kelsey circled the kitchen again, almost calm now.

Mandy watched her warily. "Um, Kelsey? I don't know if this is fixable."

"Of course it is. He has to man up and admit he screwed up. And stop trying to buy you out of your land. And move to Harmony permanently. And—"

"Whoa, wait a minute! Don't you think you're getting a little ahead of yourself?"

"Nope. It's good to have a plan. You, my friend, need to decide what you want."

"Hold that thought." Mandy reached for the phone ringing next to her. "Hello, Whimsy, this is— They hung up." She looked at the call display. "I really wish we could trace these calls. But it always shows as a blocked number."

"Did you hear anything at all this time? Sometimes you can hear someone breathe. And a couple of times, when one of us picked it up, the caller asked for you." Kelsey glared at the receiver. "Since hearing about Kevin acting so... so... underhandedly, I might have wondered if he did the calling. Except it sounds more like a woman."

She swung back to Mandy. "Anyway. We were talking about what you want."

"No, we're really not. Not much point. If he wanted me, and not only the land, wouldn't he have told me on Saturday? Instead, he let that slimeball Aaron Bridges interview him."

"You can't hold that post against him. You know what Bridges is like. He doesn't interview, he ambushes. Look at how he treated Melanie Larson and the story he printed in the *Chronicle* about her father. You think she ever gave him an actual interview? And what he can't discover through intimidation or subterfuge, he flat out makes up." Kelsey had really hit her stride now. "Which makes me wonder how much of that article about her was really true, and how much was exaggeration and innuendo."

"Well, it's no secret Kevin presented the Main Street development project to the council. Or that he approached Anderson & Anderson about buying the land, before he knew who owns it. And once he found out, he did talk to Auntie Anna."

"But you don't know for sure what he intended. Your great-aunt has always been pretty protective of you, given what happened with your mom over the years. Are you sure she didn't simply ask him what his intentions are?"

"He has no intentions toward me! Only toward the land." Frustrated, Mandy threw up her hands.

"Are you sure?"

"One hundred percent? No. But pretty sure. Kels, if there was anything else to it, wouldn't he have at least called? Tried to talk to me? Even tried to talk to Auntie Anna again?"

"Maybe, maybe not. He's the outsider here. And Harmony tends to circle its wagons around one of our own. Between you guys having that argument in public in the Foothills Dining Room, where all of your friends could hear, and the post on the *Chronicle*'s Facebook page, which everyone in town has probably read by now, his back is up against the wall. A small gesture isn't going to cut it. Not here, not for this."

Chapter Eighteen

Kevin leaned against the window frame and stared out into the night. The yellow-orange circles of light from the street lamps dotted the road and sidewalk like glowing jewels. The occasional car drove by, and the even more occasional pedestrian hurried on their way, but Main Street stayed a quiet, empty place after midnight.

His hotel suite felt quiet and empty too. He cracked open the window, hoping some sounds from below would come in with the cool, damp air. Instead, over the expected sounds and smells of the night came the yipping of Mrs. A's little dog and the faint scent of pipe smoke.

He frowned, absently rubbing the center of his chest. The yapping he expected; he'd run into Gill in the elevator with the small white furball as they rode together to the sixth floor.

The pipe smoke confused him. It didn't smell like the old, stale smoke that hung around in a hotel for years even after the smoking ban went into effect. It smelled like someone was smoking a pipe right outside his window.

He opened the window all the way and stuck his head out as far as he could. He felt like an idiot. And he really hoped no one looked up from the street.

As he turned sideways to look down the length of the building, a window in the suite next door slammed shut, closing off the yapping noise. Taking a deep breath, Kevin could still catch a whiff of the pipe smoke. *Not likely Mrs.*

A's got a guest this late. Even if she did, she wouldn't let them smoke, would she?

He didn't want to get the old lady in trouble for smoking in her suite, but he didn't want to wake up with his own room in flames because she fell asleep with a lit pipe in there either. Oh well. He'd have a word with the front desk tomorrow.

He closed the window, closed the drapes, closed out the night. And sealed himself in his room with his thoughts.

* * *

Kevin woke abruptly to a dark and silent room. Sleep had been a long time coming, and he hated jolting awake before the alarm went off. Opening one eye, he looked at the clock, then groaned and shoved his face back into the pillow. If he could get back to sleep quickly, he'd get another two, maybe two and a half hours.

He had barely dozed off when he heard a noise. Again. He heard the little yippy-yappy dog from the suite next door. How could he hear it through walls and closed doors and windows? No matter. This time, when he rolled over, he shoved his head under the pillow.

That's when he felt the poke at his shoulder, and smelled the pipe smoke again. Jeez, had the old lady fallen asleep and set the place on fire? An emergency was the only reason he could think of for someone to be in his room in the middle of the night: to wake him up and get him out. He couldn't see anyone. Between the late hour and the heavy layered curtains, the room was pitch black.

"Good, you're awake." The gruff voice accompanied another of those shoulder pokes. "You have to help her."

"Who, Mrs. Arbuckle? Can't your staff do that? Let me—"

The voice growled at him, and the unseen hand went from poking his shoulder to grabbing his bicep, pulling at his arm, half lifting him out of the bed.

"All right, hold your horses! I'm coming. I don't hear any alarms, so give me a minute to get dressed... Wait. I don't hear any alarms. Why don't I hear any alarms?" He sat on the edge of the bed and grabbed his jeans from the chair where he'd thrown them. "Why haven't you called 9-1-1?"

Kevin reached for the phone, only to have it slapped out of his hand. "No time! Fire's not here. You have to help her."

"Look, whoever you are, let me get some pants on and we can go— Hey, wait!" His unseen visitor dragged him over to the window and yanked aside the heavy drapes. "Wish you hadn't done that. I'm half-naked here."

He leaned against the wall and managed to get his jeans on without falling, then turned to... no one. There was no one there.

Had he dreamed the whole thing? No, he hadn't opened the drapes. He was pretty sure about that. And the smell of pipe smoke lingered in the air.

The gravelly voice spoke again, "Look, and see. You have to help her."

He didn't want to think about what he didn't see. Instead, he focused his attention on the view out his window. The sky was still completely dark. No cars went by at this hour. And no pedestrians.

So why did he see a flicker of movement across the street? He squinted, trying to bring the dark blur into focus.

He saw a shadow, where there shouldn't be a shadow. The near end of the opposite building held a florist shop that stayed completely dark at night. And unlike Mandy's apartment over Whimsy at the other end, the apartment above the florist stood empty. No lights there either. He should know; his suite lined up with it right across the street. He'd seen this same view every night for months.

There! He saw the movement again. This time, the small glow of light at ground level stayed on. Sort of. It didn't shine with a nice, steady glow like an outside security light (not that he thought the shop had one). It didn't even move like a flashlight would in someone's hand. It pulsated, swelling and shrinking, like a…

"Fire!" Oh shit, he saw a fire in the shop across the street.

Later, when they asked him, he didn't remember the mad dash down the stairs because calling and waiting for the elevator would be too slow. He didn't remember yelling on his way out the front door for the startled night clerk to call 9-1-1. He didn't remember racing across the street, ignoring the pain as his bare feet hit the cold concrete, stumbling when he slid on a patch of ice refrozen over a puddle.

"Mandy! Open the door! Damn it, Mandy, get out of there!" He heard the wail of sirens from the fire hall two blocks away, followed almost immediately by the roar of the engines as the trucks came around the corner. He ignored the noise, focusing on leaning on her doorbell and hammering on the outer door. Shouldn't she hear the sirens by now? And why hadn't the building fire alarm gone off?

Kevin took three steps back and looked up at her apartment windows. Still dark. Her bedroom overlooked the back parking lot, but surely she could hear the doorbell from there?

As he lunged for the door again, a strong hand grabbed his arm and swung him around. "Sir! Sir, you have to stand back. Let us take care of this." A firefighter in full gear pulled him away from the building and shoved him in the general direction of an RCMP car. "Hey, Nallos! Come get this guy out of here."

"No, wait! There's someone in the apartment upstairs. You have to get her out of there! She's—"

"We know Mandy Brighton lives above her shop. We know hers is the only apartment occupied in the building. They'll get her out if they need to. Step back and let them do their job."

The relentless grip on his arm pulled him back. Kevin stumbled away from the building and into the street. His focus solely on the door into the apartment lobby, he didn't hear the sirens give one last blip and then stop.

167

Finally, he saw the lights in Mandy's apartment go on, followed by the lobby light. The RCMP officer holding his arm turned him around; he didn't see the firefighter go into the building through the door she'd opened.

"Sir. Sir?" The cop shook his arm gently to get his attention. "I understand you were the one who called in the fire?"

"Not exactly," he replied, craning his neck to see behind himself. "I'm guessing the night clerk at the Thurston made the call, but I saw it, yes." Kevin pointed to the top floor of the hotel. "That window on the end there is mine. I saw movement, like a person, and then the glow of the fire."

"So you came running across the street, to do what exactly? You knew the trucks were on their way."

"But they all were focusing on the end of the building where I saw the fire. I couldn't hear any alarm going off inside this end. Mandy lives above her shop, and I wasn't sure she would realize the fire was in her building, I—"

"You took it upon yourself to play the hero and try and rescue the damsel in distress." The officer shook his head. "Look. I'm Officer Roger Nallos. I'm going to go over there"—he pointed to the mass of firefighters working at the fire scene—"and find out what the deal is. You, on the other hand, are going to go back into the hotel and wait."

"But—"

"No buts. You're in the way here. You can either go back on your own to your hotel room, or I can have someone escort you there. But you will go, one way or another."

Kevin bit back a heated retort. No point in antagonizing the officer. He wouldn't find anything out that way.

He turned and trudged toward the hotel, then spun back around when he heard a familiar slimy voice.

"Officer! Officer Nallos? Aaron Bridges here, *Harmony Chronicle*. I heard from a reliable source someone deliberately set the fire. Can you confirm? Did they do it for the insurance money? Is that why you're here at the home of the building owner? Will you be making an arrest tonight?"

"You can't believe Mandy had anything to do with this!" Kevin strode back to where a frustrated Nallos pushed a recording device away.

"And look, here comes the other interested party. So, Mr. MacNeal, for the record: Were you after her land? Did you set the fire?"

"Me? You sleazy son of a bitch, I had nothing to do with it!"

"Bridges, get out of here before I haul you in for impeding an investigation," the disgusted officer said.

"So there is an investigation! Can you confirm whether MacNeal here is a suspect?"

"There's always an investigation when there's a fire. Get out of here and let us do our jobs." Then he pointed at Kevin. "You too. Go back to your hotel. If we need you, we'll come find you."

Chapter Nineteen

At least they let her go back upstairs and get dressed. Mandy had managed to ignore both the sirens and the ringing doorbell. But the constant banging on her outer door drove her out of her apartment and down the stairs, ready to yell at the idiot who wouldn't leave her alone.

Except it wasn't an idiot. "Logan? Logan Wright? What are you doing here? What's going on?"

"Didn't you hear the sirens, Mandy? We answered a 9-1-1 call about a fire at the florist." Logan Wright lived next door to her friendly competitor, Chastity Howell, the owner of a tea shop a couple of blocks away. Dressed in full firefighting rig, air mask dangling, helmet pushed back on his head, he made an imposing figure standing in her doorway.

She tried to duck past him. She had to get outside and see how bad the damage to her building might be. "What? I ignored the sirens because the building alarm didn't go off. I figured the fire was down the block someplace."

"No, it was here." He moved forward, crowding her so she had to take a step back into the building. The door closed behind him and shut out most of the sound. "Fire was pretty much extinguished when they sent me down here to get you. Cops are going to want to talk to you."

Logan's gaze wandered over her with enough male appreciation to make her blush. Mandy knew he had a thing for Chastity, that he had been interested in her for as long as she could remember. Apparently interest elsewhere was no deterrent against looking. And she hadn't exactly dressed for polite company, in her flannel sleep pants and tank top and fuzzy socks.

She cleared her throat. "Logan?"

His eyes snapped back up to hers. "Sorry." He took off his helmet and scratched his head sheepishly. "Look, do you know Roger Nallos?"

"The RCMP officer? As a customer, anyway. He comes into Whimsy at least once a week. Some sort of fancy latte, and a cupcake of the month every time."

"Yeah, well, he's here and he's going to want you to come down to the detachment and give a statement. If you want to go get dressed, I can let him know you'll meet him there."

She swallowed hard. "They think I set the fire?"

"No, no!" He hurried to reassure her. "Look, it's not my place to say anything. But no, you're not under any sort of suspicion. We know the fire was deliberately set, but even if it hadn't been, there would have to be an official investigation. Since you own the building, you'll want to be informed every step of the way. So will your insurance company." He stepped back to leave. "I'll let him know you're on your way. Oh, and he sent MacNeal back to his hotel, but you still might want to go out the rear entrance."

Mandy stopped her rush up the stairs. "Kevin? Did he come out when he heard the sirens? I guess a lot of the hotel guests did."

"A lot did, sure. But he's the one who called it in. Nallos is going to want to talk to him at some point too."

That thought stuck in her mind as she went slowly up the stairs, got herself dressed, and drove to the RCMP detachment. Kevin called in the fire? How would he have known about it? She could not believe he had anything to do with setting the fire. Even though he wanted her land, she felt certain he would never try to burn the place down to force her out. Besides, even if the building burned down, she had sufficient insurance to rebuild in the same place.

By the time she approached Officer Nallos's desk, she was a nervous wreck. Maybe she should have called her great-aunt. No, no point in waking her up. Or Kelsey either. She looked at her watch. She had to be in Whimsy to start the morning baking in an hour and a half. If she couldn't leave by then, she'd have to call Kelsey and risk waking up her kids with a ringing phone.

As she considered leaving a note and coming back later, Roger Nallos appeared and sat at his desk. "Thanks for coming in, Mandy." He scrubbed his face and then ran his hands up into his hair, mumbling, "I hate this crap."

"What, fires? Look, I don't know what's going on, other than someone called in a fire at my building. Is there anything you can tell me at this point?"

"Sorry about the language. Comment wasn't about you. Yes, I can tell you some, and you can answer some questions." He rummaged around on top of his desk for a pad and pen.

"Do I need a lawyer?" Mandy asked quietly.

"Not yet. Wait, wait," he exclaimed at her sharp gasp. "That didn't come out right. Yes, you will probably need a lawyer to deal with all the fallout, but you don't need a lawyer to defend yourself, if that's what you were thinking. Look," he said, swinging his desk chair to face her directly. "Let me ask you some questions, and we'll see where it goes. Then, yeah, you might want to give your lawyer a call."

At her cautious nod, he continued, "We picked up someone running from the scene of the fire, about a block away. Idiot ran toward the firehouse and our detachment carrying a gas can and reeking of smoke. So when we picked up... this person, we didn't have to work hard to get a confession."

She'd caught the hesitation when he said "this person." So he likely knew, or knew about, this person. And since they'd caught someone running away... "So you know it wasn't Kevin MacNeal."

"Well, we know he didn't set the fire, sure. We're still trying to sort out whether he had any other involvement."

She shook her head vehemently. "No way. Not a chance. I may not be very happy with how he's handled things, but I don't believe for a second he had anything to do with the fire. What would he have to gain by burning down the building? We're well insured for fire. I carry one hell of a policy, because of the commercial ovens in Whimsy and all the baking ingredients and supplies. If the place burned down, I'd rebuild."

He nodded his head, taking notes as she spoke. "Yes, the insurance coverage came up during the confession. They also mentioned the fact Mr. MacNeal wants to buy your land but not the building or the businesses. And while the arsonist tried to connect the dots between themselves and MacNeal, no connection has been substantiated."

She started to shake. "I don't get it. This person you've got locked up, they implied Kevin wanted to burn the building down, to force me to sell? I don't believe it. You can't believe it." Mandy gripped her hands between her knees. She was cold. Why was she so cold?

Nallos eyed her as she hunkered down in the chair, shivering, then walked over to a cupboard and pulled out a blanket. "Here. I think shock is starting to set in," he said, wrapping it around her shoulders. "Better? Good. Look, Mandy, we don't think MacNeal had any direct involvement. A lot of what this person is saying doesn't make sense. But we need to chase down all the loose ends so they don't come back and bite us in the butt. So, if you're good," he waited for her nod, "I'd like to move on to the more difficult, more personal stuff."

"More difficult and more personal than almost accusing the guy I recently started dating of trying to burn down my building? Hard to believe."

"Yeah, well, wait for it." Nallos blew out a stream of air. "This is the part I hate." He rolled his pen over his knuckles and back. "When was the last time you spoke to your mother?"

"My... Oh, no. No, no, no. She couldn't have. She wouldn't! Would she?"

He shrugged. "I can't tell you what she would or wouldn't have done in the past. I haven't been in Harmony long enough to have known her, and no one talks about her except to say she's not here. I can tell you we have someone who says she's your mother sitting in a cell because she confessed to setting the fire outside the florist shop in your building."

Mandy felt her face get hot, then cold. Her hearing faded out and she swayed in the chair. She must have looked as bad as she felt, because Nallos caught her as she started to slump to the side, and yelled for someone to bring him a bottle of water.

He scooted his chair right next to hers and steadied her until the water arrived and she sipped at it slowly. "Better? I'm sorry for the shock. There wasn't an easy way to tell you."

"No, I suppose not." Mandy picked at the label on the water bottle. "Are you sure she really is my mother?"

"No, we're not. That's why I asked you to come in immediately. The insurance stuff could have waited till tomorrow. But the sooner we can make a positive ID on her, the sooner we can move forward. Look, maybe the best way to do this is to show you. Come on." He got her up and moving, blanket and all. "We've got her in an interrogation room. You can look through the glass and make the ID. Or not," he said as they went through a door and down the hall, deep in the bowels of the detachment.

She didn't watch a lot of TV, but Auntie Anna loved police shows, so she had seen her fair share. The two rooms were pretty close to their on-screen depiction: the sparsely furnished interrogation room, with a metal table and three chairs, visible from the small room off to the side through a plate of one-way glass.

Only one of the chairs in the interrogation room had an occupant. Sure enough, there sat her mother, slightly the worse for wear. Actually, Janine looked a lot the worse for wear.

Seeing her mother, seeing how much she aged between visits, always gave Mandy a jolt. Her mother had had her baby at sixteen, but Janine looked far older than her mid-forties. And hard. She looked old and hard, beaten down by life. Bitter. And yet, Mandy could tell by the way she talked and gestured to the uniformed officer standing with his back against the wall that Janine was, as usual, playing the victim. None of this, not the fire, not the attempted extortion, was her fault. Nothing was ever Janine's fault.

"Yes, that's her. Janine Brighton. I don't have a current address or phone number for her. I don't know if there's anyone to contact about her, or on her behalf."

She shivered again and turned away from the glass. "Has she tried to implicate anyone? Or did she do this all on her own?"

"You mean like MacNeal? No, not directly. She keeps saying 'they' never intended to hurt anyone, but we think she's talking about an acquaintance of hers, not MacNeal. She says she wanted to damage the building enough so you'd get a payout. That, plus whatever you got from MacNeal for selling the land, would be quite a haul."

"And since I'd now have more money than the land sale alone would have gotten, she figures I would give her a nice big chunk of it."

"Something like that, yes."

He led her back to the main area. "I know this is hard because she's your mother. We have to press charges for the arson."

"No, it's actually not hard. Maybe some jail time will straighten her out. At least she won't be able to hurt anyone or set any more buildings on fire from there."

Nallos's phone rang as they neared his desk. He lunged to answer it before it went silent. "Yeah? Send him back." He hung up and indicated the chair again. "MacNeal is here, demanding to see you. And to find out what's going on. Apparently our good buddy Bridges is posting all sorts of idiotic theories on the *Chronicle*'s Facebook page."

"Oh, man." Mandy rested her elbows on Nallos's desk and pressed her hands against her eyes. "I wish I could make him go away."

"Who, MacNeal? If you don't want him in here, we can take him into a room and question him separately."

"No, not him. Or not as much. I meant Bridges, and I know there's nothing anybody can do about him." She lifted her head from her hands and sat up straighter in the chair. "Which is better, to question Kevin separately, or to have me there too? We're not exactly on the best of terms at the moment, but I don't think he would do something like this."

Nallos stared off into the distance for a moment, then returned his gaze to her. "There's something I'd like to try, with your permission. I know you'd rather not talk to your mother. But would you be open to us putting the three of you together in one interview room: you, your mother, and MacNeal? It would give us a chance to observe the two of them together. My gut feeling is like yours, and I don't think he was involved. But maybe we can get some more information from your mother if he's in there too."

"You think it would be useful?"

He nodded and said, "Decide fast. He's coming in."

Mandy took a deep breath. Her anger at Kevin, at the way things had ended, seemed weak and puny compared to her outrage over what her mother had done. No matter how she felt about him, getting to the bottom of her mother's actions—and getting her mother out of her life—were more important. She nodded at Nallos, one sharp, decisive dip of her chin.

"Good. Don't say anything to him. I want him in there unprepared so we can see their initial reaction to each other."

She looked up, eyes bleary, as Kevin arrived, escorted by a uniformed officer. "Fancy meeting you here."

Chapter Twenty

"Look, you folks wanted me to come in. What difference does it make if I come in now or in a couple of hours?" Kevin paced and fumed as he cooled his heels in the reception area. Where had they taken Mandy?

The uniformed officer behind the desk handed him a pen and a clipboard with a form. "Sir, we do appreciate your coming in. You have to understand most of us are working on the fire investigation. When someone becomes available, they'll come and get you. In the meantime, take a seat and fill out the form." When Kevin started to speak again, he raised a hand. "The best I can do is call through to Officer Nallos for you."

Kevin stood by the reception desk to fill out the form so he could hear at least one side of the conversation. It didn't tell him much: "MacNeal's here. Send him back?"

The officer hung up and looked around, then waved over another cop. "Take him back to Nallos."

They took a silent, tension-filled walk back from reception, down a long hallway, through a door, and into a large open area containing a sea of desks. More were occupied than he expected, given the late hour. Or early hour, depending on how you were counting. Spotting Mandy sitting with Nallos at the far end of the room, he pushed past his escort and wove through the maze of furniture.

"Mandy!" Kevin dropped to his knees next to her chair. His gaze roamed over her: wrapped in a blanket, face pale, eyes haggard. "Are you okay? Were you hurt? If I thought for a minute you weren't safe with the first responders I never would have let them chase me off." He glared at Nallos. "She looks like she's in shock. Shouldn't they have taken her to hospital instead of here?"

"Kevin, stop." Mandy's hand snaked out from under the blanket and grabbed his arm. "I'm fine. Really. Just shaken up. Don't make things worse."

"Slow down, MacNeal. She's fine. In fact, we're about done with the paperwork, Mandy. If you'd rather, you can come back and file it tomorrow. Well, later today."

Even though she still had hold of his arm, she wouldn't look at him. "I'd rather get it over with. Can we finish it up within an hour or so? I need to get to Whimsy and start baking."

"Don't see why not." Nallos pulled over his keyboard and started to type. "We'll get the basics done now. If I need more from you, I'll pop into the shop later." He turned to Kevin. "You, pull over a chair. I'll get to you shortly."

Kevin let go of her hand long enough to pull over another chair, then reached out and took hold again. She didn't pull away, but she didn't really respond either. *Not good.* Contrary to Bridge's insinuations on the *Chronicle*'s Facebook page, she couldn't believe he had anything to do with the fire. Could she?

Kevin frowned, wishing he could get her out of here, and take her somewhere they could talk in private. He spoke quietly; he didn't want Nallos to hear. "Mandy, don't believe everything you read on the Facebook page. Bridges has—"

"Bridges has a lot to answer for," interrupted Nallos. "Don't worry; none of us take anything he says seriously." He finished typing, clicked something with the mouse, then locked his screen and stood. "Mandy, you ready for this? Then come with me, both of you."

She stood and shrugged off the blanket, draping it over her chair before following Nallos as he walked. "Hey, wait! What's going on?" Kevin asked as he caught up to them.

"What's going on is we're going to question a suspect. I want Mandy there to confirm or contradict their answers. Since you seem to be involved somehow in this mess, we'll kill two birds with one stone and have you in there too."

"Is that even legal? Don't you usually question people separately?" Kevin's mind raced as he hurried down the hall behind Mandy and Nallos.

"Not going to question you," retorted the officer. He stopped before a closed door and rapped twice. "In. Sit. Be quiet."

Mandy still hadn't looked at him since the first glance. His eyes on her as he followed her into the small room, he didn't really pay attention to the person already sitting until she jumped up and started yelling.

"Mandy! You have to help me! Tell them who I am. They'll let me out once they know who I am!"

"Hello, Janine," Mandy said as she took one of the seats on the other side of the table.

Kevin had never heard that flat, emotionless voice out of Mandy before. Even when they had argued in the restaurant, even when she had told him to stay away from her, she had shown more feeling.

"'Janine!' Is that any way to talk to your mother?" The older woman flounced back to her chair. "You never were one for showing me any respect."

Her mother? The person arrested for arson was Mandy's mother? He slowly took the empty seat.

The scrape of his chair drew Janine's attention. "And who is this, your current boyfriend?" She eyed him the way he might eye a particularly nasty stain on the sidewalk. "Doesn't look like much. Don't let him get you pregnant. Not until you get a ring on your finger anyway!" She smirked at her own joke, and laughed until she coughed. Nallos poured her a cup of water from the pitcher on the table.

"Thanks, hon. See, Mandy, he shows respect. You should be dating this one." She winked at the officer, who ignored it.

Instead, Nallos asked, "So you don't know this man?"

"No, why should I? I don't know everybody in this hick town. I don't live here."

"Just confirming something," Nallos replied, writing something in his ever-present notepad. He turned to Kevin. "And you can confirm you have never been contacted by

Janine Brighton? Keep in mind we can pull your phone records to confirm."

Kevin shook his head. "No, I can honestly say I have never spoken to this woman before in my life." Why would they even consider such a thing? He caught Nallos's tiny head shake before he asked, and closed his mouth without speaking.

Janine slapped her hand on the table. "Well, it's been fun, boys, but it's time for me to leave. Mandy, you'll tell them I'm your mother and they should let me go, right?"

"You've never been much of a mother, but you're the only one I've got," Mandy said. "As for letting you go, I don't think that's going to happen anytime soon."

"What? Don't be ridiculous. Nobody got hurt! The building was empty, I made sure."

"So you admit to having set the fire?" Nallos placed a hand on Mandy's shoulder to stop her from replying.

"Well, sure. I did it for you, Mandy!"

"No, Mom, you did it for you. Everything you do is always for you. And you didn't make sure the building was empty. I live above my shop, remember? Where did you think I'd be at two in the morning?"

"But you didn't answer the phone! I've been calling and calling every day for weeks now. Someone always answers the phone! Except for tonight. Tonight it rang and rang, so I knew no one would get hurt, because no one was home."

"Wrong again. My cell was off because I didn't want to talk to anyone." Mandy turned to Nallos. "We've been getting these weird phone calls, hangups or no one responding. We've all gotten them on Whimsy's line. Caller ID always shows 'Unknown number' and the phone company said they can't trace it because it's a cell. So we decided not to answer them, at night anyway when the shop is closed and the line forwards to my cell."

Finally, she looked at Kevin. "We thought they might be from you. Or Kelsey thought so, anyway. Especially after... well..."

How could she think that? "Mandy, I want to—"

"Save it," murmured Nallos. "You guys can kiss and make up later. Right now, let's give her enough rope to hang herself." To Janine he said, "Once again, to confirm. You admit to setting the fire?"

"Yes, yes, I admit to setting the fire! What's the big deal? Nothing really got damaged. Harmony's illustrious fire department got there so fast, only the flower boxes and pallets caught. I didn't even have a chance to get the actual building to burn."

"Oh, man." Mandy dropped her head down onto her folded arms on the table. "I can't believe this."

Kevin reached out and laid a hand on her shoulder. She didn't pull away, which he took as a good sign. He started rubbing slow, soothing circles on her back. "Look, do you have enough? I want to get her out of here."

"Me too!" interrupted Janine. "Get me out of here too!"

"Hang on for a few more minutes. This'll be over soon," Nallos said to Kevin. "I have a couple more questions for you, Mrs. Brighton."

"It's Ms. Brighton. Never married her father," Janine answered, jerking a thumb at Mandy.

"Okay, Ms. Brighton. First question: Since you intended for your daughter to collect the insurance on the building and then, I assume, sell the land to the developer who wants to buy it, have you ever spoken to that developer?"

"Nah. I called their office in Calgary once, but I got some snooty secretary who didn't want to talk to me and wouldn't forward my call once she found out I didn't own the land. Why?"

"We'll get there. Second question: Are you sure you don't know who this man is?" he asked, indicating Kevin.

The look she sent him made his skin crawl. "Nope. I assume he's her boyfriend, since he showed up with her here. I meant what I said, girl. Don't let him get you pregnant. Kids'll ruin your life."

Mandy stood abruptly. "I've heard enough. Do I have to stay for any more?"

Nallos shook his head and closed his notebook. "No, we have enough to file charges. I can take you both—"

"File charges! What do you mean, file charges? Nobody got hurt. Even the damned building didn't get hurt! Mandy, you're not going to let them do this to your mother, are you?"

Mandy pushed away from the table, then spun back to face her mother. "My mother? You were never much of a mother. The best thing, the only thing, you ever did for me was to leave me with Auntie Anna and Uncle Joe so many times. I'm not only going to let the RCMP press charges, I'm going to testify against you if they ask me to. I was in that building tonight! You could have killed me. You could have wrecked my shop, burned down my building." She turned for the door. "I don't ever want to see you again unless it's in a courtroom."

They all tried to ignore the hysterical shrieking that followed them into the hallway. *Thank heaven for soundproof doors*, Kevin thought when the sound abruptly cut off.

They followed Nallos back to his desk. He pointed to the two chairs. Once they were seated again, he said, "I'm sorry you had to go through that. But with a nice, clean confession before witnesses, and with her not knowing who you are"—he nodded at Kevin—"we can charge her, and now we know for sure you weren't involved."

"Well, jeez, thanks." Kevin shook his head. "Can we go now?"

"Almost. Mandy, you are pressing charges, right? I'll get a formal statement from you in the next day or so."

"We can't finish this now? But yes, I'll press charges." Mandy shook her head slowly in disbelief. "I haven't spoken to my mother in more than two years. The last time she came around, she tried to hit us up for money, first me and then my great-aunt. When we both turned her down, she disappeared again."

"I know the building is owned by a family corporation or trust or something. It probably isn't any of my business, but wouldn't she be a part of it? Why would she have to hit you up for money?"

Mandy opened the water bottle she'd been carrying through the whole ordeal, drank, and capped the bottle as she swallowed. "My great-grandfather split the ownership between his two daughters. Auntie Anna and Uncle Joe bought out her sister, my grandmother, years ago, long before my mother had me. So Janine never had an official stake in the corporation. They gave my mother some money years ago, saying it was an inheritance from her grandfather, but I think they just paid her to go away. When Uncle Joe died, he left me part of his half of the corporation and the rest went to my great-aunt. I eventually bought Auntie Anna out of the bakery and turned it into Whimsy. We both still jointly own the land and the building."

"So she was never in line to inherit anything. But she came around looking for a handout?" Nallos grabbed his pen and started taking notes again.

"She tried regularly to guilt one or both of us into giving her money. I think Auntie Anna and Uncle Joe did during my childhood. Actually, I'm pretty sure they did. I know they paid for stuff like clothes and school fees for me. I'm sure they gave her money for me too, although I never saw any of it. So as soon as I could legally walk away from her, I did.

I came to live with them, and they stopped giving her money, which didn't go over too well." She shrugged. "They helped pay when I went to school for the pastry chef program. I paid them back, and then a few years later I had saved up enough for collateral on a loan to buy the bakery. I guess my mother somehow feels since I'm making some money, I should support her. Or something."

"And that's the point we got to before you arrived. She rambled about the fire insurance settlement and money from the land sale. Which is why we were wondering if MacNeal got sucked in somehow." He stood. "Thank you both for coming in. We have enough to move forward. If I need more from either of you, I know where to find you."

He walked them out and shook hands with both of them. Mandy had already turned away toward her vehicle when Nallos caught Kevin's arm and held him back.

"Look, MacNeal, it's none of my business. But I've known Mandy for a couple years. And you heard her in there. Her mom checked out early, even before she ditched Mandy with the Lipiczkis."

"Yeah, so I gathered. What's your point?"

"My point is, our girl got used to being unwanted and left behind by someone who should have been her first and best protector. It's not only her great-aunt that keeps her here. Harmony is where she feels safe and valued. So, you have to choose. Which is more important to you, the land or the girl?"

"It's not so simple," protested Kevin.

190

Nallos smiled. "Sure, it is. If you want the girl, give up the land. Find a different piece to develop. Lord knows there's enough of it out by the highway. And then find a reason to stay above and beyond developing a parcel of land."

"Like what? Not much call for an architect in a small town, I wouldn't think."

"Have you asked around? I know Harmony Construction has their fingers in a lot of pies. Go talk to Mac. And, MacNeal, when you talk to Mandy? You screwed up. Make it right."

Chapter Twenty-One

She hadn't stopped running all day.

Mandy took the third batch of cupcakes out of the ovens as Kelsey arrived. "Girl! You have been mighty busy! Jeez, can't leave you alone for one night and you turn the town on its ear," her employee commented.

"I see you have your finger on the pulse of Harmony news, as usual." She slid the tray onto the rack and rolled it over to the walk-in cooler.

"You mean the *Chronicle*'s Facebook page? Hell, yeah! And theirs isn't the only one." Kelsey dumped her coat and purse in Mandy's office and came back to wash her hands and get started on the next batch. She looked around first at the disarray. "You really have been busy. Good thing too. They're lined up outside all the way to the corner. Want to open early? Do you have enough ready?"

"No, and no. The first rack should be cool enough to frost. If you want to get started mixing up the buttercream, you can do those while I get another batch of cupcakes in the oven. We've got fifteen minutes before we have to open, so let's see how much we can get done before we're overrun." She grabbed all the equipment from the clean end of the dishwasher and brought it back to the worktable. "I think I should call Zak in. It's his day off, but we're going to be swamped."

In the next eight hours, Whimsy sold almost as many cupcakes as they usually did in a week. Mandy called in favors to get rush deliveries from her suppliers, and even sent Zak on an emergency run to Calgary to pick up what they couldn't get delivered and couldn't borrow.

He staggered in through the back door, wheeling a handcart loaded with sacks of flour and sugar. "What's the population of Harmony, about twelve thousand? How many of them have been in here today to get a cupcake with their gossip?" He cut open a flour sack and dumped the contents into a clean rolling bin. "Has he been in yet?" He ignored Kelsey's slashing hand motion as he pushed the bin over to Mandy.

"No. And I don't want to talk about it."

"A little bird told me he started his morning at Harmony Construction's office, not at the job site. Then he went into Anderson & Anderson, and then he got in his truck and headed for Calgary."

Both women stared at him in amazement. "Where do you get this stuff?" marveled Kelsey. "That little tidbit didn't come from Facebook, did it?"

"I have my sources." Zak smirked as he wrestled a sack of sugar from the handcart and dumped it into another bin. "How's Suzette been out front, handling the masses?"

"She's been terrific, but you should go out there and give her a hand."

Kelsey slid off her stool and grabbed her water bottle. "I'll go. I want to see who's out there, who might be the source of Zak's information."

The double doors swung open and closed, open and closed, and Mandy could clearly hear Mrs. A's hearty laugh. "You pumped an old lady for information?" she asked Zak as they measured ingredients and assembled the next batch of cupcake batter.

"I most certainly did not! I didn't pump, I bribed. She's a sucker for your double chocolate with mocha icing," Zak retorted. "Wanna hear the rest?"

"Yes. No! No, I don't want to hear any more." She kept her head down, her eyes on the eggs she carefully cracked into a big steel bowl. "If he's gone, he's gone."

"Gone? Why would you think he's gone?"

"Didn't you say he didn't go to work this morning? Instead, he went to the office of the company who is, for all intents and purposes, his employer while he's here. Then he went to a lawyer. Then he drove off back to where his actual employer is located. Doesn't that sound like he is quitting the project, giving notice to Harmony Construction, breaking his contract through a lawyer, and leaving town?"

"Sheesh, way to look on the dark side of everything. I bet there's a far better explanation. Why don't you go ask Mrs. A if she knows any more than what she told me?"

Mandy stared at him for a full minute, her mind racing. Even though she and Kevin had fought over his going behind her back to her great-aunt, even though she had told him to stay away from her, surely if he intended to leave town for good he'd have come to see her? Even if it was only to tell

195

her she'd won and he couldn't buy her land out from under her?

She didn't want to believe he had left so abruptly, without saying good-bye.

She didn't realize tears fell until Zak came around the table and eased her down onto a stool. "Oh, man, I'm sorry. Don't cry! Jeez…" He looked around the kitchen wildly, as if someone else—preferably someone female—would magically appear and deal with the tears. "Sit here. I'm going to get Kelsey."

Kelsey breezed in, took one look at her, and sighed. "Oh, hon."

"He left, Kels. I thought, after last night… I thought maybe things were going to work out. Maybe he wanted me more than the land." Mandy turned her tear-drenched face to her friend. "Did you know he called in the fire? He saved my building. And he tried to save me. Logan—you know Logan Wright, the firefighter, Chastity's neighbor?—Logan said they had to physically move him from my door. But he left." She sniffed hard, then gave a watery laugh. "I guess finding out my mother set the fire, and I would still never sell, was the straw that broke the camel's back."

"Does he know you're in love with him?"

She caught her breath on a gasp. "I'm not! I can't be. It's much too soon."

"You're well on your way, then." Kelsey pulled out a stool and sat next to her. "If he really is gone, then he's an idiot and he doesn't deserve you." She rode right over

Mandy's half-hearted objection. "I don't believe he's gone, though."

"You don't?"

Kelsey shook her head. "Mrs. A said he took off in a huge hurry. He hasn't checked out of the hotel. All his stuff is still here. And yeah, he went to see Mac Berg, the big boss at Harmony Construction, but there's no rumors about Kevin quitting the project. The guys from the town hall job site have been in and out all day, and no one's said anything of the sort."

Kelsey stood and grabbed Mandy's arm, half dragging her toward the door. "Come on. We're going to talk to Mrs. A. And, Mandy? Just because your mother doesn't value you for who you are, doesn't mean no one else does."

Mandy followed a step behind Kelsey as they wove through the crowd in the front of the shop. She had to; Kelsey had a viselike grip on her elbow. She smiled weakly at the customers who greeted her even as they made way for a determined Kelsey.

Mrs. A sat in a place of honor at one of the small tables away from the front door. Judging by the crowd eddying around her, and the litter of teacups and cupcake wrappers in front of her, she'd been the prime source of information for a good chunk of the afternoon.

"Here she is, Mrs. A!" Kelsey announced. "Now you can tell her directly."

"Sheesh, Kels, a little louder, maybe?" Mandy freed herself from Kelsey's grasp and rubbed her arm. She'd probably bruise. "Sorry about this, Mrs. A."

"Not to worry, my dear!" The older woman beamed at her. She basked in her glory, with news to impart and an audience to listen. "Why don't you sit down and tell me what you already know? I'll see if I can fill in the gaps."

Mandy pulled out a chair, sitting so she faced away from the room and the crowd. "I don't know anything for sure. Zak came in with some stuff he'd heard from you, about Kevin going to see Mac at Harmony Construction instead of going to the job site. And then he went to Anderson & Anderson, and spoke to Brock, I guess. And then, well, then he left town."

Madeline Arbuckle nodded. "That's pretty much all I know. Except he spoke to Reg Anderson, not Brock." She huffed out an aggrieved breath. "If he had spoken to Brock, I could have asked Riley what they talked about. But she didn't know, because Brock didn't know."

"So... that's it? Still doesn't tell me the why part. Why he didn't go to work, why he went to see Mac instead, why he had to talk to a lawyer, or why he left town." She slowly rose and settled the chair back under the table. "Thanks, Mrs. A. I know you tried. If anyone could have found out more, it would have been you."

"Well," said Madeline, setting down her latest cup of tea and nodding in the direction of the door, "there is one way to find out more. You could ask him yourself."

Mandy whipped around so fast she nearly dumped the chair and table into Mrs. A's lap. The bells on the front door had been jangling regularly, as customers came and went. This time, though, this time when the door opened, the crowd didn't shuffle aside to let the newcomer in. This time, everyone froze, and went silent. She heard only the steamer on the cappuccino machine, hissing into a pitcher of milk.

Kevin looked a little shell-shocked as he entered and gazed around. He clearly hadn't anticipated such a large gathering, nor had he expected their focus to be on him. He stood quite still in the open doorway, peering around, obviously looking for someone or something.

She could barely see him for the crowd. Gradually, people eased out of the way. Her line of sight opened up, then narrowed down until she saw only him. His gaze found hers and never left.

He made his way through the opening in the crowd, murmuring the occasional "excuse me" or "sorry" as he stepped between and around the bystanders, his eyes still on hers. Mandy had never seen his face so blank. She couldn't tell what he felt or thought.

Kevin came to a stop in front of her. "We need to talk."

Chapter Twenty-Two

The look on Mandy's face scared him. Kevin kept his own expression impassive. He led her through the crowded shop and into the kitchen. The big room echoed, empty of people.

She came to an abrupt stop about six feet in from the swinging doors. "Kevin, it's okay. You don't owe me any sort of explanation. I get—"

"Yes, I do." Kevin circled around so he could see her face. "I've heard a lot of stuff going around today. Mostly it's true, but it doesn't tell you anything."

"Mrs. A had a lot to say, but none of it explained anything." Mandy stepped to the side and paced away from him, hugging her arms, looking cold.

He looked around and found the stools pulled up to the table. "Why don't we have a seat? You tell me what she said, and I'll tell you what it means."

She looked at him, doubt in her eyes, but she sat. "Then let's start with you not going to the job site this morning."

"Truth," he declared. "No, I didn't go to the town hall job site this morning. Yes, I did go to Harmony Construction and talk to Mac Berg. And then I went to Anderson & Anderson and talked to Brock's uncle, Reg. And then I drove to Calgary." He pointed at himself. "And back, as you can see. So that's what Mrs. A—and all those people in your shop—have been talking about all day?"

"Pretty much." She dropped her gaze to the table. "I guess, anyway. I stayed back here most of the day." She shrugged. "I didn't want to face anybody. I didn't want to think about whether you were gone for good, or whether you were coming back."

"I don't blame you. But you didn't really think I would leave without talking to you, did you?" He had to make her understand, to believe he wouldn't ever hurt her. An awful lot depended on making her understand.

"Honestly? I couldn't be sure, after last night. My crazy mother tried to burn my building down! You had every right to run for the hills."

Kevin grabbed the stool next to her and sat. "You think I left because of what your mother did?"

"I hoped you left because of what my mother did. Because if she wasn't the cause, then I must have been."

He reached for her hand, grateful when she didn't pull away. "It wasn't you, it was me." They both winced. "That didn't come out right. I had some things to take care of, okay? Better?"

She didn't say anything, and he figured he had better start talking. Fast. "Nallos said some things to me last night, and they made me think."

"Nallos?" She looked up at him, startled.

"Yeah. He asked me one question in particular. He asked me which I valued more, you or your land. And then he gave me good advice. He told me I'd screwed up, and I had to make it right."

"You didn't screw up last night. They told me you tried to save me. You—"

"Not last night," he interrupted. "But I definitely did screw up. I should never have talked to your great-aunt about selling the land, especially not behind your back. I should have respected what you told me when you said you didn't want to sell, and left it alone. You weren't the only person who kept telling me how much you belong here. But I was the only person who didn't see it."

He cleared his throat. "I didn't want to see it. I wanted... Well, I wanted to make a mark on Harmony. And I didn't see you already had."

"So... what does that have to do with what happened today?"

"So, today. Today I didn't go to the job site. Instead I talked to Harmony Construction about other opportunities. They've been dangling a couple of projects in front of me for weeks now. But I got caught up in this one, redeveloping Main Street, and I kept telling them no, not now. Last night, when Nallos said 'choose,' I finally figured out he was right."

He squeezed her hand. "I can't have both, Mandy. I guess I thought you were stuck here, rather than you really wanted to be here. So if I talked up moving Whimsy to Calgary, you'd see things my way. You'd sell me the land, I could get my name on the redevelopment project—and then you and I could pick things up when I got back to Calgary. When you walked away from me in the Foothills Dining

Room, I figured you had chosen living in Harmony over me. I realized last night you would never be happy with someone who wanted you to give up your dream so I could have mine. And I would end up not respecting you if you did."

He cleared his throat. "This morning I went first to Harmony Construction and talked to them about some of the housing developments they've got on the go and in the planning stages. They want me to sign on to do the neighborhood planning as well as the house designs."

"But you work for a firm in Calgary. Will your company agree to keep you here longer than the town hall and community center projects?"

"Let me tell you the rest. After I left Mac I went to see Reg Anderson. He's representing the owners of some land out by the highway. I wanted to get the specs and the bottom-line pricing. And then I drove to Calgary to talk to my boss."

She went very still, then took a deep breath. "You're telling me you're going to develop somewhere else? Not on my land?"

Kevin turned her hand over and laced his fingers with hers. "I don't know if the investors will go for it. It's kind of a toss-up. The land is cheaper, but since it's not right downtown, they might have to rethink the anchor tenants. But I told them in no uncertain terms that this land, your land, was no longer an option." Kevin took a deep breath himself. "And then I quit."

"What? Why?"

"Because there's more opportunity here than I thought possible. Because starting my own company is something I've been thinking about for a while. And I figure who can help me better than someone who already runs a successful company, so successful she's thinking about a major expansion?"

"You mean… me?"

He watched the emotions flit over her face. Disbelief, followed by hope, followed by… He couldn't put a name to the last one, the one that settled in and shone out of her eyes. "Yes, you. And I quit because I don't want to live in Calgary if you're living here."

Kevin brushed a wisp of hair from Mandy's face with his free hand. "Look. I don't know what the future holds for us. But I want to see where this can go. I want us to have a chance, Mandy."

The tears pooling in her eyes spilled over. "I'd like that, Kevin." Something between a hiccup and a laugh escaped her. "So, would you say all of this happened on a whim?"

"Well, I don't know if I'd call it a whim. But I decided pretty quickly, yes. Once I figured out what I wanted, what was important, it— What?"

She fizzed with laughter. "Think about how this all started. I entered the silent auction prize on a whim. I accepted your invitation to dinner, before the silent auction dinner, on a whim. Kelsey and Zak kept cheering me on, because I never do anything on a whim. So now you're telling me you've quit your job, and you're moving here, on a whim?"

"I guess I am." He laughed right along with her. "So, what do you say, Mandy?" He stood and pulled her up with him, holding her close. "Will you take a chance on us making a go of it?"

Mandy wrapped her arms around him. "You're really staying?"

Kevin rested his chin on the top of her head and breathed her in. Her familiar scent of vanilla and sugar filled his nose, comforting, arousing. "I'm staying. There's a future here for me, one I couldn't see till you and some other folks showed me how. There's a future for us too. I want to see where it goes. I want to see where we go."

"I want to see where we go too." She sighed against his chest and snuggled closer. "I wasn't sure about you, not at first. But that didn't stop me from falling for you."

His heart gave a tremendous thump before settling into a pounding rhythm. "I wasn't sure about you either. And it didn't stop me from falling for you."

Mandy pulled back enough to look up into his face. "This doesn't sound like it's on a whim anymore."

"It may have started that way, but no, it's not ending up that way," he confirmed. "It's sounding more like a plan."

"Oh? And what might that be?" she asked.

He leaned in to kiss her. "I plan to marry you," he murmured against her mouth.

Mandy ended the kiss with a resounding smack. "How do you feel about purple?"

Kevin laughed and dove in for another kiss, this one longer and deeper. And so, on a warm March afternoon, in the middle of the big kitchen at Whimsy, they started to plan.

THE END

BOOKS IN THE THURSTON HOTEL SERIES

Find them all at http://www.thurstonhotelbooks.com/

ACKNOWLEDGMENTS

My thanks to the other Thurston authors, for contributing countless hours to inventing and sharing characters, to planning settings and plotlines, to completing the extensive research required, and to contributing your valuable input in making the hundreds of decisions needed to achieve the unprecedented series continuity we strove for. A special thank-you to the continuity editors who read every book, many times, to ensure that continuity. Hopefully, readers, we've only goofed a few times, and with our apologies.

Thank you to the many friends and family members who were sworn to secrecy while we planned and plotted and sweated blood to create this series.

A special thank-you to the very talented Su Kopil from Earthy Charms Designs for crafting twelve excellent covers that tie into the series perfectly. We couldn't be happier with your work. Please check out her website at http://www.earthlycharms.com to view her designs. Thank you to Ted Williams, the line and continuity editor for the series.

And an extra big thank-you to Jessica Gardner, my fabulous editor. Next time, I'll give you more warning!

ABOUT THE AUTHOR

Win Day is a storytelling geek who loves to read and write about strong men and savvy women. *On a Whim*, a stand-alone warm contemporary romance in a collection of twelve books by eleven authors, is her first published novel.

Born and raised in New Jersey, Win moved to Canada after working as an engineer in an overseas oil refinery, where she met her husband, Tom. The two have been married for thirty-six years, and have two sons who are all grown up and living on their own. Win and Tom currently live in Calgary, Alberta, Canada.

A member of her local chapter of Romance Writers of America, Win divides her time between building custom WordPress websites for authors, and writing both fiction and nonfiction. She learned long ago that she needs both the technical and the creative to keep her brain busy and her heart happy!

When she isn't writing or working on a website, Win enjoys traveling to warm places (she's solar powered!), cooking (and eating!), and curling up on the couch with a good book. And listening to all sorts of music.

Win believes that everyone deserves their Happy Ever After. And if you're not living yours right now, duck into a book. Someone else's story can give you the hope you need, and show you what's possible.

FIND WIN ONLINE

Writing website: http://www.windaywrites.com/
Visit and sign up for information about new releases!

Web development company:
http://www.creativeimplementations.com/

Facebook: https://www.facebook.com/WinDayWrites/

Twitter: https://twitter.com/WinDayWrites
(@WinDayWrites)

Email: Win@WinDayWrites.com

64208752R00123

Made in the USA
Charleston, SC
22 November 2016